JUST FOR BOYS™ Presents

The Chimpanzee Kid

A NOVEL BY
RON ROY

Clarion Books

TICKNOR & FIELDS: A HOUGHTON MIFFLIN COMPANY

New York

*This book is dedicated to those humans, like
Harold Pinto, who have compassion for animals,
and who act on that compassion.*

R.R.

This book is a presentation of **Just For Boys**™,
Weekly Reader Books. Weekly Reader Books offers
books clubs for children from preschool through high school.
For further information write to: **Weekly Reader Books,**
4343 Equity Drive, Columbus, Ohio 43228.

Published by arrangement with Clarion Books,
Ticknor & Fields, a Houghton Mifflin Company.
Just For Boys and Weekly Reader are trademarks of
Field Publications.
Printed in the United States of America.

Library of Congress Cataloging in Publication Data
Roy, Ron, 1940-
   The chimpanzee kid.
   Summary: Considered to be something of a misfit by his classmates because
of his interest in animal rights, Harold finds a friend in the new boy in class
who agrees to help him in his secret plan to free a caged lab chimp.
   I. Children's stories, American. [I. Animals—
Treatment—Fiction. 2. Friendship—fiction] I. Title.
PZ7.R8139Ch 1985   [Fic]   85-3755
ISBN 0-89919-364-1

One

HAROLD LIKED GERBILS better than hamsters. Hamsters play at night. Scurrying around in their pine chips and doing loop-de-loops on their exercise wheel, a pair could keep a guy awake all night. So, two years ago when Harold's father asked what he wanted for his eleventh birthday, Harold had asked for gerbils.

The next day Willie and Tammy came to live in Harold's bedroom. He brought his old aquarium up from the basement and washed it out carefully with mild soap and hot water. The clerk at the pet shop sold Harold's father a huge bag of sweet-smelling pine chips for the aquarium bottom. Harold filled and hung the water bottle and set a small dish of food on the pine chips. Then he gently placed Willie and Tammy in their new home and covered the aquarium with a wire-mesh screen.

Harold had named his pets after his two favorite country singers, Willie Nelson and Tammy Wynette, thinking he'd have little baby country-singer gerbils in a few weeks. But either he had two boy gerbils or two girls, because they'd lived in his room for a little over two years now and neither one had given birth.

Willie and Tammy were still pretty small even for gerbils, but when Harold's father brought them home, they were the size of walnuts. Harold had played with them for days. That was before his dog died, and old Max had been jealous. Harold remembered hearing Max howling away in the backyard pen while he and the gerbils crawled all over his bedroom floor.

Lying in bed thinking about all this stuff, he counted the seconds until his mother would knock on his bedroom door. Thursday. About a month left before summer vacation started. One year and sixteen days since his father walked out. One year and twenty-two days since Max died. Harold missed his father. His stomach still felt like he'd swallowed something hard when he thought of him. Why hadn't his father at least called him or sent him a postcard?

Now and then Harold would be sitting in school or walking home from the library and a picture would flash into his mind. The picture was always the same: They were at this sandy place somewhere on Lake Ontario. His father and mother would be standing ankle deep in the lake. Jeans rolled up, laughing, his father was getting ready to toss a stick into the water. Max would be flipping around like crazy, his tail smacking the water and his tongue hanging, just waiting for Dad's arm to move.

In his daydream Harold wasn't in the picture. He would be standing out of range, watching his parents and his dog. It was always sunset. Soft yellow halos surrounded their bodies, making them look as if they were about to fade away.

The knock made him jump, wiping out the Lake Ontario scene the way a cloud can suddenly block out the sun.

"Harold? It's almost seven thirty."

"I'm up, Mom." He wasn't, but he knew if he didn't start moving he wouldn't make homeroom by eight fifteen. If he was late for homeroom he'd get sent to the office, thereby missing his first period, study hall. Harold needed the study time to put the finishing touches on his English report.

He threw the covers back and rolled to a sitting position in the middle of his bed. He slept in running shorts although he wasn't a jogger. Pajamas made him too hot, and his underwear was too tight. With his mother liable to burst in on him, he dared not sleep nude. The green shorts had been his father's, so they made Harold look even littler and skinnier than he was. He stood under five feet, the shortest seventh grader at Levy Middle School.

"Harold, are you up?" His mother was racing around out there, making tracks between the bathroom, her bedroom, and the kitchen. "I can't hear you in there."

Harold answered by yawning loud enough to make Willie and Tammy perk up their little ears in their aquarium across the room from his bed. He jumped up, shucked his shorts for underwear and jeans, tugged a brush through his red hair, and scrounged around for a clean shirt. He looked out the window, grabbed his jacket off the floor, kicking stuff out of his way as he dressed. The room looked the way it always did: a place for everything and everything in its place—on the floor.

He lifted the top of the aquarium and dropped in a fistful of gerbil food. He checked the water level in the bottle and decided it could wait to be filled. "Have a nice day, Tammy. Willie, you be a good boy." Harold gave each gerbil a little pat on the head. He made sure his typed report was still in his bookbag, checked himself quickly in his mirror and headed for the kitchen.

Coffee smells made the room seem cozy. A bowl containing a few bananas, oranges, and apples stood next to a large box of Nutri-Grain cereal in the center of the round, butcher-block table. Two places had been set. Harold's mother stood at the small kitchen window, her back to the room, sipping from her coffee mug.

Her name was Tamatha, but her best friends called her Tammy. Harold had three Tammies in his life. His mother had teased him about naming a gerbil after her, but his father knew Harold had named his pet after the singing star.

His mother turned and ran her eyes up and down, checking to make sure he was really dressed. Harold dropped his bookbag on the floor. He grabbed an apple and started chomping. In the past year, he had become an expert at finding ways to avoid talking to his mother or looking directly at her.

No one had asked him how he felt about the divorce. No one had asked him anything. His father was there one day, and then he was gone. Harold went through a tornado of

4

confusion, grief, and crying that made him sick to his stomach. How could they do this to him? How could a family of three lose a third of its members and still be a family?

After the crying stopped, the anger came. Anger at his father for leaving. Anger at his mother for not making his father stay. She could have stopped him, Harold told himself.

"It's only eight," his mother said. "Have some cereal?"

Harold's mouth was filled with Granny Smith apple. He shook his head, flicking his eyes in the general direction of where his mother stood. She was dressed in her usual outfit: skirt and blouse proper enough to wear at the bank, sporty enough to play golf in after work. The color today was medium blue, like her eyes. Her hair, a few shades paler than Harold's carrot color was pulled back and held in place with combs made out of hand-carved turtle shell. His mother was pretty good-looking, Harold had to admit.

"I'll be shopping after I leave the club tonight." She turned and poured herself more coffee from the Morning Maid pot on the counter. "Anything special I can get for you?" She smiled over her coffee mug.

There were plenty of things Harold could think of: his father back home again; the kind of family they used to be with nobody missing; a dog like Max out there in the pen, leaping around with a tennis ball in his mouth. But to ask for these things was out of the question. Kids who were mad at their mothers didn't ask for stuff. Harold had decided a little over a year ago that he'd never ask for anything again. If you got things and loved those things, they disappeared on you.

5

He looked up at the clock, pretended he thought he was going to be late, and bolted for the door. "Wait a second." His mother dug something out of her skirt pocket. His eyeglasses. "You won't be able to read your report without these." She set her coffee down and held the glasses out to him.

Harold stood in the breezeway door, half in the kitchen and half out. He knew she was staring at him, but he was looking somewhere over her head, at a crack in the kitchen wall he'd once heard his father say was growing an inch a month.

His mother slipped his glasses into the pocket of his jacket. "We don't seem to have much time. . . . I mean, with me at the bank now, I can't be with you as much. I wish we could spend some time together if . . ."

Harold felt his face freeze over. Whenever she got that embarrassed sound in her voice he knew what was coming. She wanted to talk about Dad, the divorce, and how Harold should really try to make friends and not let the divorce interfere with his life. But the divorce was interfering with his life. It had cost him a father. Harold couldn't forgive his parents for that. It wasn't as if his father had died. He had just . . . gone away.

So Harold had learned to clam up, tune out, shut down all systems. The divorce was definitely interfering. "I really gotta go, Mom," Harold said. He escaped, ran through the backyards and lots that would take him to school the fastest way.

Two

THREE HOURS LATER he sat in English class waiting for Patty MacFarlan to finish reading her report. A lot of the kids, the guys especially, were whispering while Patty read about her Scottish grandparents and how they came to this country and opened a clothing store in Albany, New York.

It was almost lunchtime, and everyone was hungry. Harold's stomach rumbled about ten times. He wondered if Patty heard it, or thought he was doing it on purpose to give her a hint.

He was next after Patty. The guys would probably really groan and pretend Mr. Stanley was starving them to death. Harold knew he wasn't exactly the most popular kid in class anyway, and now they'd blame him for being late for lunch. Tough. He'd worked hard on this report, and he was going to read it and get his A.

Patty sat down. Her girl friends clapped like mad. Mr. Stanley told her she'd done a fine job. Patty blushed and messed around with the stuff on her desk.

"Harold? You have a little over thirteen minutes." Mr. Stanley sat in the back of the room, next to the fish tank. "Think you can read your report before our friends back here faint from malnutrition?"

Everybody liked Mr. Stanley. He was a hard teacher, but fair, and he had a neat sense of humor.

Harold stood up and carried his report to the front and laid it on Mr. Stanley's desk. Then he turned and tugged on the bottom of the world map. The world disappeared like a window shade. In its place hung a large drawing of a chimpanzee. Harold had hidden it there after school the afternoon before.

The drawing was as tall as Harold. He had used three sheets of the art teacher's largest drawing paper, taped together. Across the bottom, in his best printing, Harold had written the words: THIS CHIMPANZEE NEEDS OUR HELP.

Somebody let out a laugh, the kind that explodes because you've been trying to hold it in. "That a self-portrait, Pinto?"

A few kids snickered, until Mr. Stanley said, "Boys, ease off."

Harold used a yardstick as a pointer. Holding his report in his other hand, he began reading, starting with his title: *"The Chimpanzee, A Vanishing Friend. By the time you and I are grandparents,"* Harold read to his English class, *"there may not be one wild chimpanzee living on earth."*

8

He read slowly, pronouncing every word clearly. He wanted to make sure everyone got his message. Chimpanzees are an endangered species. Man is taking their habitats and building housing complexes, airports, shopping centers. Scientists buy baby chimps from poachers and lock them in cages.

The spitball made a *thwack* sound as it hit the chalkboard behind Harold's head. It stuck wetly there for a few seconds, then fell into the chalk tray with a soft *plop*.

Even wearing glasses, Harold hadn't seen the small flying wad.

Nor had Mr. Stanley, who was concentrating on Harold's words.

" . . . *and these chimpanzees are being mistreated. They're being denied their rights!*" He tapped his drawing of the chimp with the yardstick. *"Right here in Watertown, New York, these endangered animals are being used for experiments. I'd like your help to—"*

"Is this an English report or are you runnin' for office?" someone called out.

The voice came from the back of the room where the jocks huddled in their clique. The leader, the one the rest orbited around like planets around a sun, was Todd Sims.

But Harold knew the wisecrack hadn't come from him. It came from Billy Merck, who was holding out his palm for the congratulatory "slap me five, man" ritual.

Todd ignored the offered palm and the hoots of the boys around him. He kept his eyes on Harold, and pretty soon the guys quieted down.

Harold was used to taking flack from these nerds. He'd known them since first grade. All except Todd Sims. He'd shown up at Levy a couple of months ago from New York City. It had taken him two days to become the most popular guy in seventh grade.

The class took advantage of Harold's embarrassment to pile up books and stuff papers into backpacks. In five minutes, if Harold would ever shut up, their actions seemed to say, they'd get to eat lunch.

"Hold it, class. I'd like to give Harold time to summarize, since he didn't have a chance to finish." Mr. Stanley strolled toward the front of the room and leaned against the doorjamb. He flashed one of his lopsided grins. "Harold? One more minute okay?"

Harold Everett Pinto scratched at his messy hair. Everyone was staring at him. Feeling flustered, he studied the top page of his report. He'd spent weeks doing the research, agonizing hours typing on his mother's old portable.

Someone groaned. "Ya only got fifty seconds left, Pinto. Let's go!"

Harold drew himself up to his full four feet seven and a half inches. "Laboratories all over this country are using chimpanzees for weird experiments. Chimpanzees are endangered. They shouldn't be locked in cages. They should be free, like you and me. I think we should make it a class project to—" He stopped. They were laughing.

"Like last month when you asked us to get the farmers to stop using pesticides? What happened to that class project, Harold?" a voice hollered above the sounds of shuffling feet and scraping chair legs.

"Yeah, and what about those poor baby seals you

collected a buck a kid for?" someone else yelled. "What happened to all them bucks, Harold?"

The bell saved him from having to answer. Twenty-four kids shot out of the room. Harold folded his report with trembling fingers. He shoved his glasses higher on his nose. The clang and smash of locker doors in the hall gradually quieted.

Harold rolled the chimpanzee drawing into a thick cylinder and wiggled a rubber band over one end. He felt like throwing the drawing on the floor and jumping on it.

"That was an excellent report, Harold." Mr. Stanley helped him get the rubber band in place. "I could tell you did a lot of work on your research."

In spite of feeling rotten, Harold smiled, just barely. Mr. Stanley had that effect on kids. "They sure didn't like it."

Why do you think so?"

Harold stuffed his report into the pocket of his purple fake-satin jacket. He didn't have an answer. He stared at the patches it had taken him hours to sew all over the jacket back: BAN THE BOMB, SAVE THE WHALES, ARMS ARE FOR HUG-GING. At one time or another he'd tried to get the kids in his classes to join him in fighting the injustices the patches represented. He shrugged into his jacket and tugged on the zipper.

"Harold?"

"They don't like me." Harold removed his glasses and shoved them into a pocket. He swiped at the slab of hair falling over his eyes. "None of 'em do."

"I do." Mr. Stanley tugged on his beard while he stared at Harold. He was famous for holding kids in his gaze till they

11

looked away. His eyes were like wet brown marbles. "Do you think it's fair or accurate, for that matter, to accuse people of not liking you because they don't agree with what you're saying?"

He was also great at asking questions a guy couldn't answer. Is that what I'm doing? Harold asked himself. No. Merck the jerk hates me, and I hate him.

"I gotta go, Mr. S." Harold shuffled past his teacher's feet. He wouldn't look at him, but he knew he was still getting zapped from those eyes.

The halls were empty. He stopped at his locker and swapped the rolled-up picture and his bookbag for gym stuff and lunch. He thought about cutting gym. It was softball this month, and nobody wanted him on their team anyway. "We gotta take the Pint? He can't hit nothin" Coach!"

He was tempted, but Harold decided he'd better not cut again right away. His mother would find out from the office, and gym was her big thing.

He slipped his cassette player over his belt and adjusted the earphones on his head. Willie Nelson warbled into his ears.

He slammed his locker door and locked it, then headed for the lunchroom. He didn't have to worry about finding a seat; there were always plenty left for loners. Harold told himself that he preferred eating alone.

He put his glasses on and surveyed the cafeteria. The air smelled strongly of macaroni and cheese. The noise of a couple of hundred filled mouths trying to talk made Harold thankful for his earphones.

He saw an empty table and headed for it. Past the cliques that ate together every day: the artsy group in their dark turtleneck sweaters; the newspaper gang with their long hair and serious faces; the jocks in the corner, yelling and tossing food around.

Harold slid onto a bench and shook his bag open. One Twinkie, one apple and a flat, tinfoil-wrapped mound fell out. He smelled the tinfoil. Egg salad again. He wished his mother wouldn't insist on making his lunches for him. But he had to admit that what he found in his bag was usually better than the stuff they served.

The lunchroom monitor motioned for Harold to remove his earphones. He stuffed them inside his jacket and took a bite of his sandwich. Mayonnaise city. Harold wished he'd stopped in line for a milk. His mother used about a gallon of mayo for six hardboiled eggs. His throat screamed for something wet.

"Hey, Harold, good report."

Harold looked up, surprised to hear his name. Todd Sims was leaning against the end of the table. He was Harold's age, but that's where any resemblance ended. Where Harold had skinny, Todd had muscle. What God had left off Harold in height, he'd given to Todd. Eyes the color of faded jeans. Pepsi-ad teeth. They were smiling down at Harold now.

He felt a little funny. Sims didn't usually just walk up and start talking to people.

"No kidding, I thought it was interesting. Where'd you learn so much about chimpanzees?" Harold stared at a glob of oozing mayonnaise. What did Sims want with him? Did he expect him to kiss his track shoes the way the rest of the guys did? He crushed his tinfoil into a ball.

"There are other things in life besides making dunk shots," Harold said. He toyed with the Twinkie, but he had no appetite suddenly. Even to him his words had sounded unnecessarily rude. Todd's comments had been friendly. He didn't deserve to get blasted.

Feeling guilty, Harold took a deep breath. "Look, I'm sorry," he said, looking up. "I just . . ." But he was talking to himself. Todd Sims was gone.

Harold grabbed his Twinkie and hurried out of the cafeteria. A few kids were standing around waiting for the bell. Sims had disappeared.

It had been hard enough making himself apologize. But to discover that no one was even listening made Harold's face hot with embarrassment.

Maybe Mr. Wood was right. In the weeks after his father left, Harold had spent plenty of time in the principal's office explaining his antisocial behavior. It was mostly stuff like answering teachers back. Did he want to talk with the school psychologist, Mr. Wood had asked. No way. He didn't need the school faculty feeling sorry for him. "In that case," Mr. Wood had told him, peering up at Harold over his glasses," why don't you see if you can exercise a little more restraint. Soon."

At his locker again, Harold twirled the combination. He had four minutes till gym started. To heck with it. He wasn't going. He didn't need ten laps around the track or hearing everyone yell at him when he struck out. Which he did, often. Between his dumb glasses and too-long hair, he couldn't see the ball, let alone hit it. He wouldn't miss the jokers in the locker room, either, throwing soap around and snapping butts with wet towels.

He slipped through a side door and headed across the teachers' parking lot. Please, don't some teacher decide to get something from his or her car right now. He walked as if he had a legitimate reason for going home at twelve thirty. Maybe he should go into town instead. Forget it. His mother might be on her lunch break and spot him cruising around. If he went home, he wouldn't see her till after five. One thing about having a mother who's a bank teller: you always know when she'll be home from work.

Harold checked the sky. Sunny. A few cumulus puffballs looking like cotton glued on blue velvet. Golf weather. His mother would stop by the club to play nine holes.

He could picture her after, chatting with Cora and Mavis, her buddies. Laughing at her "silly slice." But Harold knew his mother. While she "joked" about her game, she was serious. Her slice cost her points.

Tammy Pinto ached to be the best woman golfer at the Watertown Golf and Tennis Club. She'd receive a trophy and a year's free membership. But first she had to beat Ruth Goldberg, who had been numero uno at the club for years.

Since Harold's father left, his mother had turned into a golf nut. Weekends. After work. *Exercise,* she called it. Harold thought she was lonely. He didn't know if grown-ups felt the way kids did, when someone died or just took off. She had never talked about how she felt since Harold's father left. All she wanted to talk about was how Harold felt.

She looked like nothing bothered her at all. But you never know with adults. They keep all sorts of things to themselves. Like divorces.

For about the millionth time, he wondered if his father would ever come back. Wondered why he had left in the first place. And how they had kept their unhappiness such a big secret from him.

At first, when he was still talking to his mother, he had asked. "He's gone, Harold. He's not coming back." Her words returned as clearly as if they had been spoken yesterday. "You'll have to accept this the way I have. Forget him and go on with your life."

She certainly had. She'd thrown out every personal item he'd left behind. Even pictures. She'd cut her hair and taken up golf. Gotten a job. Her mail came addressed to Ms. Tamatha Pinto. Harold couldn't figure out why she had kept the last name. He liked it that his mother was still a Pinto because when his dad came back she'd have the right name. But that was pretending, and he knew it.

Harold hadn't gone on with his life. He couldn't. It was stuck, snarled like a cassette in a tape deck. School was lousy, he had no friends, he couldn't talk to his mother.

If he'd known where his father had gone, he'd have written him a letter. But he didn't think his mother would tell him even if she knew. Anyway, he wasn't planning to ask her.

It was Thursday. Maybe things would get better over the weekend. They have to, Harold joked wryly to himself as he came to his street. They sure can't get any worse.

16

Three

THE HOUSE LOOKED deserted, as usual. Like most of the others on Clancy Street, it was a small house attached by a screened breezeway to a one-car garage.

The gray paint needed scraping and a fresh coat. One white shutter hung crookedly. Dark green flower boxes waited below the two windows, flowerless. Harold's mental camera flashed a picture of him sitting on his dad's shoulders as a little kid. It was springtime, a flower planting day. His dad sticking baby flowers into the flower boxes, Harold patting the dirt around the small roots. His mother, laughing, was standing inside the window telling Harold to be careful not to get dirt in Daddy's eyes.

Harold shook his head and the picture faded. He was

standing on the porch of the same house. But everything had changed. The lawn was overgrown with bright green May grass. He sighed. I'll mow it tomorrow.

He wiggled his key out of its hiding place behind the mailbox and let himself in. The mail was all for his mother, except for Harold's monthly issue of *LEAP*. A couple of years ago he'd sent three weeks' allowance to a team of biologists in Alaska. They were trying to find a way to prevent whales from tangling themselves in fish nets and drowning. Ever since, Harold had received monthly copies of their newsletter.

After a quick run to the bathroom, Harold dumped his school stuff on his bed. He made sure Tammy and Willie were okay, then headed back to the kitchen. He was hungry. Because of Todd Sims, he hadn't eaten his lunch.

The freezer compartment door on the refrigerator swung open when he stepped on the pedal down by the floor. He shoved aside cartons of frozen pies and rock-hard vegetables to find the ice cream. Or what was left of it. He kicked the door shut and sat at the table with a spoon and a nearly empty carton of Chunkee Chocolate.

The first bite froze his back teeth and the roof of his mouth. The pain shot up toward his brain, making his eyes water. Waiting for it to go away, he thought of the scene with Todd in the cafeteria.

Had Todd really been trying to be friendly? Or was he just taking pity on the class nerd? He had said he liked the report. No one else had, except for Mr. Stanley.

I worked hard on that report, Harold thought. He took another bite of ice cream, smaller this time. He flashed back to himself when he was six or seven. He'd been snake-happy in those days. Bringing them to the table hidden in his pockets, stuff like that. Then it was baby birds, or squirrels whose mommies got shot by hunters, even an owl once.

Harold smiled. His dad had built him cage after cage, till the basement looked (and smelled, his mother kept reminding him) like a small zoo. She gave Harold all the vegetable leavings and scraps of meat. But she stayed out of the basement.

Later, Harold found himself attracted to bigger, more exotic wildlife. Seals, Bengal tigers, whales, alligators—all being slowly wiped out by humans. Harold didn't want to live in a world where the only lion was a stuffed one.

He began spending his free time in the library, poring over the books in the animals section. An article he saw in the *National Geographic* got him started on chimpanzees.

Then the librarian showed him how to use *The New York Times* microfilm machine. That's where he learned about the lab in Watertown and a few other things. Chimpanzees were endangered, yet they were being captured as babies in Africa, brought to America, and forced to live in cages, sometimes for their entire life. They were kept separate from other chimps, so they couldn't play or mate. Their only communication was with scientists, who had things other than playing in mind for the prisoners.

Harold flopped the cardboard lid down and chucked his spoon into the sink. He smashed the empty ice-cream carton and tossed it into the yellow trash basket next to the stove.

The telephone book lay on the shelf next to the cook-books. Harold carried it over to the table and opened to the *L* section. He knew from *The Times* article that the name of the lab was LAPS, but he didn't know what the letters stood for.

LAPS wasn't listed. He turned back a page and looked under *La* for laboratory. Bingo: Laboratory for Primate Studies. Chimpanzees are primates, like humans, apes, go-rillas, all the monkeys. The lab was on Turnback Road.

Harold stared at a fly on the screen door, banging its hard little head trying to get out. So the place really did exist. He pictured scientists in long white coats cackling as they per-formed their grisly experiments. Behind the lab, a huge furnace belched out putrid-smelling smoke, the only thing left of the chimps lucky enough to die and be cremated.

No. The article had said that the staff at LAPS was de-voted to the chimps who lived there. Clean cages, fresh food and water. Harold felt pretty sure *The New York Times* wouldn't lie. But still.

Those chimps were there against their will. They should be chasing each other up trees somewhere in Africa, not sitting in little cages, staring into space.

But when Harold had told his English class about the lab they had laughed and given him a hard time. Maybe he hadn't followed through with the seals or the poisonous pesticides. Three months after he'd sent the dollars to Save the Seals a thank-you letter had arrived, along with some stickers and a poster. With this as evidence, he had tried to interest the kids in writing letters to state senators. No takers.

He washed his spoon and stared through the window

into the backyard. The dog pen stood empty. If he squinted his eyes and willed his mind-camera into action, he could still see Max out there. Lying with his paws crossed in front, like a small lion, golden in the sun.

Harold's mother had turned the fifty by twenty feet chain-link pen into an enclosed putting green. Official, velvety grass, the whole bit. She'd even added the little sunken cup your ball was supposed to fall into.

She spent almost all of every weekend hitting golf balls around in the cage, across grass as smooth as velour. Amazing. She actually looked forward to playing in a cage. But at least it was her own choice.

Harold wondered what it would feel like to live in a cage, like the chimps he'd seen in *The Times* pictures. Having your food and water slipped through a small door. Never seeing your family. Like prisoners.

But the chimps hadn't committed any crimes. And they didn't have lawyers to defend them against the people who wanted to put them in cages. Even murderers had lawyers!

Harold wasn't a lawyer, but maybe he could visit the prisoners. He could go to the LAPS place and ask to be taken on a tour. His tax money was probably supporting the place anyway. His mother's tax money, but still.

He stopped in his room for his cassette machine and a different Willie Nelson tape. He thought about leaving his mother a note, then changed his mind. He'd be back before she got home from the club.

In their aquarium, Tammy and Willie were going nuts leaping and diving under the pine chips and squeaking like crazy. Harold smiled and knelt down so he could look at them, eye to eye. "Look," he whispered. "I have something I have to do. I can't play now, okay?"

But he reached in and tickled Tammy's side. She stopped squeaking and sat up on her hind legs perfectly still. She loved to get stroked. Willie jumped on Harold's hand, expecting to get lifted out for a romp in the bedroom. But Harold took his hand away and carefully fitted the screen top back on the aquarium. "See you guys later."

His bike lay in the garage where he'd left it yesterday. There was no danger of its being run over. His mother's Subaru sat out in the weather all year. The car's once shiny silver paint had turned a dull gray. It matched the house.

Harold raised the garage door. It slid noisily along the track and rattled to a stop. A trapped sparrow shot past Harold's shoulder to freedom. Harold aimed his bike down the driveway.

In a few minutes the residential section of town lay behind him. He headed for Turnback Road, on the west side. He knew the area; Max's vet had his office out there. In the last weeks of the dog's life, Harold and his mother had driven Max over these roads about a dozen times.

Before Max died, Harold had always thought he wanted to be a veterinarian. Getting paid to fix up hurt animals.

He changed his mind when Max's vet told Harold and his mother that Max should be put to sleep. "He might live another six months or so," old Dr. Henry had said. "But he'll be in pain. Your dog is almost twelve years old. This is really the kindest thing to do."

The scene was forever a part of Harold's mental photo

album. His mother was wearing jeans and an old shirt; she had been gardening that day. Max lay on the slick tile floor, his head on his front paws, paying no attention to the vet's words. The sweet odor of disinfectant hung in the air. Harold smelled it again whenever he thought of Max's last day alive.

He rode in shade. Last month's heavy rains had forced the leaves. Turnback Road was a cool, leafy tunnel. The late May sunlight sliced through the trees, dappling the road with splashes of pale light. Birds flitted from one side to the other, carrying bits of this and that for their new nests.

Willie Nelson sang about lonesome cowboys, with Harold humming along. I'm on a mission, he told himself, aiming his front tire at the yellow road stripes. Those chimps need me!

The only real chimp he'd ever seen was in a circus his parents had taken him to as a little kid. The chimp's trainer had decked him out in a white sailor suit with a cap and tiny blue sneakers.

The chimp rode a miniature bike, did backflips, wiggled his hips inside a chimp-size Hula Hoop. Harold had laughed and clapped along with everyone else. Now, thinking back, he realized how disgusting it was to force an animal to act like a clown.

Tigers weren't put on earth to leap through burning rings. Elephants weren't meant to stand on their hind legs and wave silly little flags with their trunks. How would animal trainers like it if they were forced to perform stupid tricks in front of an audience of wild animals?

Turnback Road was long and curvy. Harold saw no signs and no buildings. Just trees displaying pale green leaves and an occasional dirt road leading who knew where.

Then he saw it: a white sign nailed to a post. The word LAPS had been painted in bold, black letters. Underneath, in smaller letters, Harold read three more words: DO NOT ENTER.

He braked and hopped off his bike. Beneath his jacket, his shirt stuck to his back. When he slid his earphones to his neck, his skin felt hot.

He silenced Willie's voice and dropped the bike kickstand. There was no breeze under the canopy of trees. The air felt like warm, wet cotton. Birds yattered all around him, invisible but loud. Everything smelled damp and new.

A dirt road snaked away from Turnback, disappearing in the thick growth. A trickle of sweat slid down Harold's neck.

Should he go in? He felt his jacket pocket. The report was still there. If anyone stopped him he'd just whip out the papers. I'm working on a report for English, he would say. I need information about chimpanzees in captivity.

Go for it, he told himself. He wheeled his bike into the bushes and leaned it against a tree, then stepped back. The bike was practically invisible from a few feet away.

He took a deep breath, then started up the long dirt road.

Four

A CHIPMUNK SKITTERED across the road. Its reddish tail stood straight up like a furry exclamation point as it vanished into the bushes.

A large bird called out, then crashed away into the trees, still yapping. Harold felt his stomach muscles tighten. What was he afraid of?

He placed his feet carefully on the road to avoid rattling the loose pebbles and gravel. Because the sun was almost directly overhead, Harold's shadow appeared monsterlike: huge shoulders topped by a massive head.

Then he heard another noise. This was no bird call. The sound was part screech, part laugh. It had come from up ahead somewhere and not too far away.

Harold's hands felt clammy. His mouth went dry. He hesitated, then continued walking slowly. The dirt road ended abruptly and turned into a clearing.

Sunlight poured over a large grassy area almost as well cared for as his mother's putting green. The lawn was round, sloping gently upward and surrounded totally by forest.

Three buildings hugged the far edge of the woods along the back of the clearing. The large middle building reminded Harold of his school: all sturdy-looking brick with tall windows. Azalea shrubs, a few already in pink or white bloom, prettified the cinder-block foundation.

A smaller brick building stood about a hundred yards to the left of the first. This one had no windows that Harold could see. There was a door, though, facing the larger building.

He heard the noise and noticed the girl at the same time. She came out of the house. An ordinary white house with bright red shutters and a porch with a fancy railing. It looked weird standing next to its brick companions out here in the woods.

She didn't notice Harold. He stood watching her climb onto a girl's yellow ten-speed bike. He didn't know what to do.

The screechy noises shattered the quiet scene. They were louder this time.

The girl looked in the direction of the small brick building. "Quiet, Benny." Her voice floated clearly across the open lawn. "I know Sam fed you, so don't try to fool me."

She bumped her bike across the lawn. She had Max's hair, gold with flashes of red. She flipped it over one shoulder so she could see where she was heading.

Should he hide? Too late. The bike was only about twenty yards away and headed right for the dirt road where Harold was standing.

When she noticed him, the girl jerked her handlebars to the left and dropped both feet to the ground. She started to smile, then seemed to change her mind. "Who are you?"

He felt totally foolish, like a little kid caught with his hand in the cookie jar. He said, "I'm Harold Pinto."

The girl leaned back against her seat, staring, waiting.

Harold felt himself turning red. Where the heck was that little speech he'd practiced a few minutes ago? Heat crept up the back of his neck like a centipede. "I saw the sign—"

"Which says Do Not Enter." She was about his age. Designer jeans, a light blue hooded sweat shirt with CARRIE printed across the front. A few freckles rode her cheeks like small bugs.

"This is private property, you know."

Carrie wasn't a smiler.

"Yeah, I know." Harold tried to sound as if he weren't trespassing. "I'm doing a report." He yanked the folded papers from his pocket and held them up as proof.

"What kind of report? How come you get to be out of school?"

Harold felt like asking her why she wasn't in school. "It's about chimpanzees. In captivity, how they act and stuff. I know about LAPS."

"A lot of people do."

This was not a friendly girl. "So, can I?"

As if to answer, the strange noise shrieked across the lawn. *Harch-harch-cheeee!*

Harold had heard similar sounds in old jungle movies on TV. "What's that?" he asked.

"Benny, trying to get more food out of us. He's our oldest chimp. We—Look, you really can't stay here. My father doesn't like people hanging around, so—"

"Can I see him?"

She shook her head, making her hair fly around her face. "He had to go into town to—"

Harold laughed. "No, I mean Benny. Can I just take a quick look? For my report?"

"My father doesn't let strangers near the chimps. Some of them are dangerous. We can't take the chance that someone might get hurt." Carrie looked at a slim watch on her wrist. "Look, you really have to leave now, okay?" She looked as if she would pedal over Harold's toes if he didn't move. "I have to get back to school, and it's almost a mile."

Harold jammed his report back into his jacket pocket. Somehow he knew better than to push too far. There were other ways to see the chimp who made the loud noises. He walked beside her as she rode her bike carefully over the bumpy dirt road.

So where do you go to school?" he asked. Levy was a lot farther than a mile.

She kept her eyes on the road. "Leafbrook Country Day. It's private."

Everything in her life must be private, Harold thought. He'd heard of her school. Rich kids went there. Or kids whose parents didn't think they could get a good education at plain old Levy Middle School. Maybe they were right. Most of the time Harold didn't think he was learning anything.

"I go to Levy. It's pretty boring." Harold wondered what it would be like in a private school. Did the kids still have to take gym? He sneaked a look at Carrie's face, mostly hidden by her hair. "What's it like where you go?"

"It's hard, but I like it. We have real small classes, and the teachers are nice. I want to be a scientist like my father. How about you?"

"What do you mean?"

They were at the end of the dirt road. The girl braked her bike and looked at Harold. "What do you plan to do? You know, when you grow up. For a job."

Harold hadn't spent a lot of time planning the rest of his life. It seemed to take all his energy just to get from one day to the next. He kicked at a small stone and sent it skittering across Turnback Road. "I haven't decided yet," he said to Carrie.

Who wasn't listening. She was checking her watch again and looking for cars. "I have to go. How'd you get here, anyway?"

"I hitchhiked. Do it all the time." Harold fiddled with the earphones circling his neck. "It's a lot faster than riding a bike."

Carrie's eyes widened. They were really blue. "My father would *kill* me!"

29

Harold watched her ride away, hair flying, feet pedaling, off to become a scientist. Like her father. Who wouldn't kill her if he caught her thumbing a ride. Fathers don't hurt their kids, Harold told himself. At least not some fathers.

He stepped into the trees and removed his jacket. He tied it to the seat of his bike. He was going back to those buildings, and this time he wouldn't pop out of the woods like some lost Boy Scout.

This time nothing would stop him.

Five

FROM THE WOODS where he stood hidden, Harold heard low barks and grunts coming through the open window of the small brick building. Because the window opened onto the back of the building, it hadn't been visible to Harold from the dirt road.

He'd been standing in a clump of sassafras trees for over five minutes. There seemed to be no activity at LAPS. He saw no people, heard no sounds other than birds and the noises through the window.

He stripped a few of the hand-shaped leaves from one of the trees and stuffed them into a pocket. Crouching, he sprinted out of the woods and flattened himself against the bricks. He was James Bond. Hostages were being held inside this little prison. His bomb, disguised as a Willie Nelson cassette, would blow this wall into dust. He'd enter through the smoke and debris. . . .

A low thumping noise from inside broke into Harold's fantasy. He edged over to the window and peaked in. The sharp smell of urine made him wince.

A row of three metal cages lined the wall opposite the window. The cages were about five feet tall. The three small doors were locked with sturdy-looking padlocks.

The cages stood six or eight inches off the floor on big rubber wheels. A long sheet of plastic had been spread on the floor, under the cages. A puddle of urine colored the plastic. The sour odor reached Harold at the window.

A large black male chimpanzee squatted in the middle cage. Small dark eyes stared at Harold out of a sad, intelligent-looking face.

He was taller than Harold had expected, at least five feet or so. His arms were thick and hairy, longer than his legs. He had big ears like the fake rubber ones Harold had once worn for Halloween. The chimpanzee was nearly bald on top. Long, yellowed teeth showed between rubbery, black lips.

The chimp's hands hung loosely, resting on the cage floor. They looked almost like human hands, only much bigger, and they were covered on the back with coarse black hair, like the rest of his body.

Suddenly he began to rub his forehead against the wire on the front wall of his cage. He never took his eyes off Harold's face in the open window.

Nothing Harold had read in the library had prepared him for this. Studying about caged animals had helped him write his report. But seeing a real chimpanzee behind thick wire, a prisoner waiting out his sentence, this hit Harold like a punch.

He felt angry, and he felt sad. What had this chimp done to be treated like this? Nothing, except to be born.

Harold tapped one fingernail on the window ledge. "Hi," he whispered. "I'm Harold."

The chimp turned his back, showing Harold his calloused rump. The cage was so small that he could take only a few steps in any direction. A pail of water stood near the front next to an empty food dish. The whole cage was constructed of strong-looking wire mesh, even the floor.

"Hey, Benny, turn around and talk to me." Harold tapped the wood again. "I want to be your friend." He felt a great urge to get inside that cage and hug the chimp the way he used to hug Max. He didn't know why, but he didn't feel a bit afraid.

Benny sat down. He turned toward Harold and scratched one ear with a long sharp fingernail.

Harold dug out the crumpled sassafras leaves. "I brought you something." He rubbed the leaves between his palms, releasing a sweet smell.

Benny shuffled to the front of the cage and peered through the wire again. He said something that sounded to Harold like *Who?*

Harold grinned. "I told you; I'm Harold."

Something heavy fell on Harold's shoulder. The same something spun him around and whomped him up against the bricks.

33

"And just what do ya think you're up to, sir?"

Harold couldn't answer. He'd almost swallowed his tongue. The old man holding him against the wall had skin like a crumpled brown paper bag. His breath smelled like kerosene. Dark, suspicious eyes darted from Harold's face to the sassafras leaves in his trembling hand.

"Well, sir? Do ya talk?"

Harold felt numb where the man's bony fingers pressed into his shoulders. "I . . . I'm visiting."

"Benny don't get visitors, sir." The man relaxed his hold. Harold almost slid to the ground. His legs felt like cooked spaghetti.

"I'm waiting for someone." Harold searched his brain for something to tell this old coot that made sense. "She's supposed to meet me," he said. "I guess she's late. Maybe I'll just lea——"

"And who would that be, could I ask?" The man backed off slightly and folded strong arms against his scrawny chest. Curly white hairs peeked over the frayed edge of a sorry looking undershirt.

"Carrie," Harold lied. "She's supposed to help me with some homework." He felt two small rivers of sweat snaking down his underarms.

The man looked at his watch. "No school today?" he said slyly.

"I got out early. To work on my project." Harold nodded toward the window. Benny hadn't uttered a sound. Probably listening to every lie I'm telling, Harold thought. "I'm doing a report on chimpanzees for English class." He didn't bother to show this guy the folded-up proof.

The man drew his lips together till they almost disappeared. Then he smiled broadly, showing a row of teeth too pearly white to be real.

"Did you try up the house?" The man jerked his head in that direction.

Harold's mind raced. "No. I . . . uh . . . I'm supposed to wait here. She's gonna introduce me to Benny. She's getting him some food. A little snack."

Harold had never told so many lies all at once. Why didn't this guy just take off? If Carrie did show up, Harold figured he'd end up in jail, like Benny.

The man squinted one eye. "Benny don't eat between meals. Carrie knows better, sir."

"What does he eat?" Changing the subject always worked with his teachers.

"Thought you did a report on these things?" The old guy was grinning like a fool. "Special stuff we call monkey chow. Sometimes fruit. Fingers when he can get 'em." He held up his right hand, as broad as a catcher's mitt. The index finger was missing to the second knuckle. He waggled the stump in Harold's face.

Harold felt slightly sick. He'd run out of things to say.

"That's why we lock the cages. And why trespassers ain't welcome. Benny's mean as a rat." The man looked over Harold's shoulder, through the window. "Been here about a year now. Before that, out west someplace, in another cage. Before that, who knows? Had every 'speriment done on 'im they can think of." He tapped his stumpy finger on the windowsill. "Right, old Ben? He'll be glad when it's over," he said to Harold.

35

Harold stared through the window. "Are there other animals here? He's not the only one, is he?"

"Only chimps. Other building's filled with the dang things. Benny's out here 'cause they're finished with 'im."

"What's going to happen to him?"

The old man stripped the bark from a thin twig and used one end to pick at his fake teeth. He sucked the stick and shook his head. "Should put'em to sleep, this old. Out of their misery. Benny here—"

"Kill him?" Harold almost shouted. "After they did all those experiments? That's not fair!"

The old man glared down at Harold. "What's fair, sir, ain't none of your business." He turned and strode away, toward the other buildings. Over his shoulder he said, "Find Carrie and don't bother Ben. He's had enough botherin'."

Harold watched until the old man unlocked a door and disappeared into the other building. He turned back to the window. Benny didn't look mean, just sad. He slumped in a corner of his cage, staring into the distance.

"Hey, Benny, want to be friends?" Harold rested his arms on the windowsill. "I could come over after school. Would you like that?"

Benny turned his head and wrinkled his black lips as if he were trying to say something. Little grunts came from his throat. He picked at a red sore on one arm.

"I have to go before that old guy comes back," Harold whispered. "But I'll come back, I promise." He waved, then turned and walked back into the woods the way he had come.

Benny let out one loud scream. Harold stopped, listening. He wondered if the scream was meant for him.

Twenty minutes later he whipped his bike into his driveway. He was puffing, dying for a cold drink.

A lime green MG with the top down sat in the driveway, bumper to bumper with a blue Audi. His mother had brought Cora and Mavis home. Her best buddies.

Harold knew the scene. First they'd practice putting in the dog pen. When it started to get dark, they'd throw together some food. Gossip, a lot of laughs, then a huggy good-night.

Harold would spend the evening in his room. He liked Cora and Mavis, but they were always asking him a lot of stuff he didn't feel like talking about. School, friends, sports, even girl friends. Harold had the feeling they were somehow trying to fill in for his missing father. Fat chance.

He left his bike in the garage and slipped into the kitchen. The golfers were out back. Laughter floated through the window over the sink as Harold gulped a glass of water.

He peeked through the yellow curtains. The women looked like sisters. They all wore their hair short and pulled back. Their faces were tanned already from all the sun they got at the club. They wore bright shirts and short skirts, revealing muscular legs. Rubber-spiked shoes covered funny little socks with colored balls at the heels.

Harold's mother was positioned for a fifteen-foot putt. Feet spread apart, shoulders dropped slightly, head bent.

Plunk. Harold had known it would go right in. His mother was good.

"Eat your heart out, Ruth Goldberg!" Cora yelled. Harold's mother laughed and caught him looking through the curtains.

"Harold Pinto, I'd like to see you, please."

Trapped. How had she found out about gym class so soon? The gym teacher must've called. Arnie Altman hated Harold. But he loved his favorites: anyone who could throw a ball through a hoop or into the end zone.

The three women trooped into the kitchen, bringing in smells of perfume and the minted iced tea they had been drinking. Harold dropped into a chair and tried to disappear.

Mavis winked at him. "You're in trouble, sweetie."

"What did I do?" Harold felt his mother watching him, so he kept his eyes on Mavis.

"It's what you didn't do." His mother rinsed the glasses in the sink and wiped her hands on the back of her skirt. "You've promised to do the lawn three days in a row, Harold. I pay your allowance on time, don't I?"

She began pulling salad things out of the refrigerator. Cora smiled at Harold. He shrugged his shoulders, flashing a look that said, I give up, I'm caught.

His mother turned and aimed a cucumber at him, pretending it was a six-shooter. "No lawn, no supper, okay, kid?"

"Okay." He headed for the garage, concealing a grin. So she didn't know about gym class. Relieved, he pulled the lawn mower out of the garage into the backyard. He flipped it over and began yanking beards of dead grass out of the blades. Through the window he heard dishes and silverware striking the counter top.

"Your kid is so quiet," Cora said. "What does he do with himself? Hobbies? Any pals?"

Harold knelt where he was, perfectly still, and listened.

"He doesn't talk to me," his mother said. "Since Hank left we've hardly had a civil conversation." There was a pause. "I try, but he seems so angry. I don't know what to do. Any ideas?"

"It takes a while," Mavis said softly. "Boys miss their dads. Keep trying, honey."

"I plan to," Harold's mother said.

He stood up and turned the lawnmower over. As he reached for the rope that would start the engine, he looked through the window, straight into his mother's eyes.

Six

BILLY MERCK STOPPED reading. He looked up at the class, grinning nervously. His face was the color of strawberry ice cream. "Any questions?" he asked.

A few snickers came from the back of the room. Harold knew Todd was back there and wanted to turn around. But he sat in the front, and that would mean facing the rest of the class. So he watched Billy squirm.

His report had been pretty bad. Billy had done it on UFOs, but most of his information sounded phoney.

Mr. Stanley tried to cover the embarrassed silence. "Class? Any questions for Billy?"

"I have one." Harold felt everyone look at him. "Where'd you do your research?"

"Whaddaya mean?" That got a laugh, and Billy turned even redder.

The room became uncommonly quiet. Everyone figured out that Billy had, most likely, done no research at all.

"Thanks, Billy. Good job." Mr. Stanley walked up front and clapped Billy gently on the shoulder. "Leave your report on my desk."

On the way down the aisle, Billy glared at Harold. "You're dead, Pinto," he muttered.

The lunch bell broke the tension in the room. Friday afternoon with two classes to go. The room exploded into a racket.

"Have a good weekend, Mr. S."

"Don't do anything I wouldn't do."

"You don't do nothin' anyway, donkey ears!"

Laughter, the noise of books being jammed into book bags, chair legs scraping across wood floors, and the classroom emptied.

Harold waited in his seat. If he saw Todd on the way out, maybe they'd walk to the cafeteria together. But Todd left in the middle of a group. He didn't look at Harold.

Harold grabbed some books for weekend homework. So now Sims would probably never talk to him again.

Mr. Stanley began clearing his desk for his next class. He looked tired. A fly buzzed the room. It found the transom over the door and escaped.

"Anything wrong, Harold?" Mr. Stanley twiddled a yellow pencil between his thumb and forefinger. Staring the Stanley stare. "Everything all right at home?"

Harold shifted his weight. Outside some kid yelled for a long pass. Everything at home is great. Only nobody's there. He stole a look at his teacher. "Everything's fine," he said.

"Why did you embarrass Billy a few minutes ago?"

"He laughed at my report yesterday." Harold didn't look up.

Mr. Stanley dropped the pencil. He let out a sigh and walked to the windows. He gazed out at the parking lot, drumming his fingers on the sill. "Harold, do you have any buddies?" He turned around and leaned back against the radiator.

Why was everyone always asking if he had any friends? Max had been his friend. And his dad. Where were they now? Friends go away. "I gotta get going," Harold said.

Mr. Stanley shoved himself away from the windows. "Have a good weekend. Hey, where's that report? You shot out of here yesterday without leaving it on my desk."

"I'll bring it on Monday." Harold didn't quite make it out the door. Mr. Stanley dropped a hand on his shoulder.

"You might tell me to mind my own business, but why don't you try to make some pals? There are a lot of nice kids in this school."

Harold thought of Todd again and how he'd insulted him yesterday. Embarrassed, he focused his eyes on the pink trout leaping for a lure in the center of Mr. Stanley's necktie. He mumbled something and backed out the door.

The halls were empty. Everyone was eating lunch or at sixth period. Harold's sneakers slapped softly on the tiles.

Mr. Johnson came around a corner, shoving a pile of green sawdust with a push broom. The smell of the chemicals reminded Harold of cotton candy.

42

Mr. Johnson smiled. " 'Lo, Sonny." He called all the kids Sonny or Missy. He'd been sweeping floors at Levy for about a hundred years.

Harold said hi and thought of the old guy at LAPS. Then he thought of Benny, locked in a cage, waiting to die.

He made a decision. Since everyone was so hot for him to make friends, he would. Benny would be his friend. Benny looked like he needed a friend, anyway.

At his locker he exchanged books for lunch. He felt excited. If he got caught, what could they do? Lock him in a cage too? He slammed his locker door and headed for the cafeteria.

The place sounded like a monkey house. Harold selected a bunch of apples and bananas from the large bowl near the cash register. Mrs. Peever eyeballed him over her glasses. "Going on a picnic?"

"Yeah, sort of." Harold gave her a dollar bill, pocketed the dime change, and walked out of the cafeteria. He thought he saw Todd sitting with his friends, but he didn't do anything about it.

He shoved what fruit he could into his lunch bag. The rest bulged the pockets of his pants and jacket. He kept his eyes straight ahead as he left the school through a side exit.

He'd cut two days in a row now. Guilt rode on his shoulder all the way home. But he felt better by the time he'd transferred the fruit to his backpack, said hi to his gerbils, and aimed his ten-speed toward Turnback Road.

Benny looked like a hairy Buddha. His black belly rested between thickly muscled thighs. The big toes on both feet stuck up at ninety-degree angles from the rest of his toes.

One arm lay across his lap. Harold saw a small bloody place near his elbow. Benny picked at the spot with a long, curved fingernail. But he showed no real interest in the sore. He gazed through the wire of his cage at something a thousand miles away.

Through the open window, Harold watched Benny swipe at a fly darting around his bloody arm. When Harold set his heavy pack on the window ledge, Benny turned his head. His small black eyes opened wider. The fingernail stopped scratching.

Harold had sat in the woods for quite a while before approaching the window. He'd seen one man, and not the old one he'd run into yesterday. The man had entered the main building about five minutes ago. Like yesterday, a warm silence hung over the three buildings.

"Hey, Benny, remember me?" Harold kept his voice low and his ears alert. "I brought you something." He unzipped the pack and held up a banana.

Benny went wild. He began shaking the wire, screaming like something from a horror movie.

Harold snatched up his pack and ran. He crawled into the bushes with his heart thudding. Hiding in the woods, he listened to Benny's shrieks. Surely everyone around the joint would come on the run.

No one came. In a few minutes Benny quieted down. Harold started breathing again. He stood and peeked through leaves into Benny's window, about twenty feet away. The chimp was sitting again, scratching his arm and staring into space.

Harold forced himself to stay put for another few minutes. He slipped his lunch bag and the fruit inside his shirt and jacket, leaving the pack where he could collect it later. Then he ran toward Benny's building again.

He counted to sixty, then placed both palms on the windowsill and hoisted himself inside.

Seven

He landed on a cement floor. Benny stared at his visitor. Please don't start screaming again, Harold prayed.

Benny looked even bigger up close. His droppings filled the room with a sour smell. No wonder the window was left open, Harold thought.

He took advantage of Benny's quiet mood to look around. He saw gray cinder block walls, a sloping cement floor with a drain in the center, gray cabinets over the sink. To his left, the door was painted to match the cabinets.

Two large plastic trash barrels stood side by side near the window. On the side of one, the words MONKEY CHOW had been stenciled in black paint.

A few mops and brooms stood in a corner. Mixed in with the handles Harold noticed a long wooden pole, taller than the others. A curve of thick wire had been fastened to one end, like a claw.

Benny shuffled to the front of his cage. Harold began to wonder if he was wise, standing so close to the cage. Could Benny break out of that place?

Deciding he was safe, he stood and watched the chimp for a long time. The whales and seals and whooping cranes still needed saving, but Benny was more real for Harold than any of those animals. He felt strangely different, as if he were starting some new phase of his life. The feeling was a little scary.

"Be a good chimp, okay?" His whisper sounded loud in the small room.

Benny stood on bowed legs. Large hands gripped the cage wire. Black fingers like hairy sausages hung through the mesh. He tilted his head, making him look curious.

Harold could hear his breathing, deep and raspy as if he had a stuffed-up nose. Benny tipped his head the other way and rubbed his ear.

Harold laughed. "You're listening to the music!" He turned up the volume on his cassette just a little, letting Willie's voice float into the room.

Benny stretched to his full height, at least six inches taller than Harold. He bounced on his legs like a 150-pound baby.

Harold reached inside his shirt and pulled out one of the bananas.

"Now don't go nuts like you did before." He tiptoed across the room and slipped the banana through the wires a few inches from Benny's huge hand.

Benny snatched the banana out of Harold's fingers. In seconds it was skinned and in his mouth. Whole. The skin landed between his hairy feet on the wire floor of the cage.

Harold peeled the next one. This time Benny took it gently. He crammed it sideways into his mouth. His teeth looked as if they could crack coconuts. Harold quickly drew his hand away. He liked his fingers just the way they were.

Benny kept his eyes on Harold's hands, as if he knew they might produce another treat.

"You still hungry? Don't go getting sick on me." Harold fed him the other bananas and all three apples. Benny chewed up cores and all. And waited for more.

"That's it," Harold said, "all gone." He still had his own lunch to eat, but he felt too nervous to enjoy it. Instead, he checked out Benny's food barrel. He pulled the lid off the container. The stuff looked like what Max used to eat: big brown chunks that smelled like medicine and looked worse. No wonder Benny had wolfed down the fruit.

Willie's voice cut off with a sudden click from the recorder on Harold's belt. Benny shook his cage and hooted, loud.

"Keep it down," Harold whispered. "I'm not exactly an invited guest in here." He ejected the tape, flipped and reinserted it, then hit the Play button. After a few seconds of static, Willie was singing again. Benny had watched Harold's every movement.

Harold was beginning to feel more nervous. He'd been in the room about ten minutes. He stuffed the banana peels into his lunch bag and shoved the whole thing inside his shirt.

Only one piece of evidence remained. "Hey, Benny, how about tossing that banana peel out here," he asked.

Benny scratched his belly.

"I gotta leave," Harold pleaded. "Let's have the peel."

Benny stuck a finger in one nostril.

Harold remembered the pole. He got it from the corner and aimed the hook end toward the cage.

Benny howled then threw himself into a corner of his cage. He sat there, arms wrapped around his head, rocking and making soft noises through bared teeth.

He's afraid, Harold realized. "I'm not gonna hurt you," he said gently. "See? Just slipping this thing through the wire . . . hooking that nasty peel . . . There, all done."

Benny continued rocking until the pole was once more standing in the corner. Harold rolled the peel into a damp ball and stuffed it into his pocket. He looked around for other evidence of his visit. He thought the place looked the way he'd found it. "I gotta go now. But I'll come back, I promise."

Benny stopped cowering in the corner. His hands fell into his lap. He watched Harold move toward the window.

Harold climbed through and dropped to the ground. As his feet struck the grass, Benny let out a holler. Harold ran into the trees. He turned up the volume on his cassette player and clapped the earphones on so he wouldn't hear Benny's yells.

He felt elated, weak, and a little giddy. He'd gotten inside and no one had come near the building. If anyone had, he figured he could've jumped through the window and run as soon as he heard a key in the door lock.

Harold came back. Except for one day when it rained, he visited Benny every day after school the following week. He brought fruit, shelled peanuts, even a head of broccoli he hoped his mother wouldn't miss.

And he stopped cutting classes. If he got caught, he'd have detention waiting at the end of the day instead of Benny.

They became friends. Harold arrived around three fifteen and waited in the trees until he felt sure that Benny was alone. Then he slipped through the window, his shirt stuffed with goodies.

After a few visits Harold no longer noticed the smell of chimpanzee dung. They ate together, listening to tapes. Harold was increasing Benny's knowledge of country music. He brought Tammy Wynette, Merle Haggard, Conway Twitty, all the greats.

He never stayed longer than fifteen minutes. By then he was jumping at every little sound from the woods outside the building. And he was careful to clean up any messes they made while eating. Benny turned out to be very neat, Harold thought.

He figured out that Benny got fed in the morning, then again for supper. He felt pretty sure no one came near him during the day. The picnics Harold brought were mainly fruits and vegetables, but now and then he slipped a special treat into his pack.

On Friday he showed Benny his first bag of M&M's. "It's our anniversary," he told Benny. "We've been friends for one week."

He poured a little pile of the colored candies into one hand and stepped near the cage.

Benny reached his thumb and one finger through the wires. He gently picked a green candy and put it in his mouth, making a sucking noise. Harold laughed.

He ate them all. When the bag was empty, Benny made a sound that Harold figured meant, What, no more candy? When Benny left his hands on the cage wire, Harold stroked one of the long, hairy fingers. The hair felt coarse, not at all soft like Max's fur.

Harold daydreamed about opening Benny's cage so they could play together. It was hard to have a friendship with someone in a cage. But the cage was securely locked. And he didn't know what Benny would be like without wire around him. He tried to imagine himself in Benny's situation. What did caged animals think about all day?

It was time to leave. On Fridays, Harold's mother expected him to start dinner. He looked at Benny. Benny stared back. It was getting harder to end his visits. He figured it got pretty lonely for the chimp in this place. Did anyone stop in to keep Benny company on weekends? Harold wondered about the girl he'd met, Carrie. Was she Benny's friend, too?

"See you later," he told Benny. "Don't take any wooden fingers." He climbed through the window. Before jumping to the ground, he waved good-bye.

Benny had moved to the back of his cage. He sat huddled on the floor with both hands covering his eyes.

That image stayed with Harold as he rode home on his bike. It wasn't fair. Chimps didn't stand a chance.

He'd read that poachers caught the babies by shooting the mothers first. They died clutching the babies in their arms.

The article in *The Times* said some baby chimps arrived at labs in the United States half dead from fright and malnutrition. Some even had BB shot embedded in their skin.

What would it feel like to have your mother shot while she was holding you? To be yanked out of her arms and stuck in a cage? Did chimpanzees have the same feelings about their parents that human kids do? Harold wondered if Benny remembered his mother and father, if he still missed them.

From his research he knew that captured baby chimps had their chests shaved and stenciled with numbers so the scientists could tell one from another.

The average caged chimp spent fifteen or twenty years in captivity.

Harold read that lab chimps were usually healthier and lived longer than those in the wild. They were kept in sanitary conditions and had regular checkups. But they were prisoners serving life sentences.

By the time Harold reached his house, a plan had begun to form in his head. He sat on his bike in the driveway, stunned by the idea. It was so beautiful and so scary that he actually had goose bumps on his arms.

He threw back his head and laughed out loud. Somehow, he promised himself, Benny would have his freedom. He, Harold Everett Pinto, would break Benny out of his cage.

Eight

THE THOUGHT MADE him dizzy. He felt warm all over, like when he sneaked a few sips of his mother's wine. It was a crazy idea. Totally nuts. How could he get away with it?

He left his bike in the driveway, up near the garage door. Inside, he dumped Benny's leftovers into the trash and went to his room. He played with Tammy and Willie on the floor. They seemed happy to be out of their cage. Would Benny feel the same way? He put the gerbils back, then lay on his bed. When he closed his eyes, he saw Benny's face through the wire mesh.

Could it work? The cage looked solid. He bet they locked that window at night. The door was locked all the time, he felt pretty certain.

Keys. The scientists would have keys. How many worked there, anyway? Harold had no idea.

He got up and wandered through the house. There had to be a way to get Benny out of that cage and the building. He poured a glass of milk and drank it while staring out the kitchen window.

Max's pen took up almost half the small backyard. A forgotten golf ball sat in the middle of the perfect grass.

"That ball is Benny," Harold told his milk glass. "The cage is locked. No keys. How do I get 'im out?"

Dynamite? No way. A crowbar? Harold put his glass down and raced into the garage. The usual stuff hung along the walls on rusty nails: gardening equipment, a few old baskets and burlap bags, ice skates that didn't fit anymore. No crowbar. No tools at all. His dad must have taken that stuff when he moved out.

Harold kicked a snow tire and walked back into the kitchen feeling beaten.

The guys at school would call this another of his causes. Wait a few days, Pinto will move on to something else. But this isn't the same, Harold argued silently. The seals and pesticides were different. Benny is . . . *personal* is the word that came to him.

He took a handful of cookies into the backyard. He separated one with his teeth and scraped the vanilla frosting into his mouth. Leaning his head against the pen, he stared at the white ball through the wire.

The answer came to him as if flashed on a TV screen.

How do you get into a locked cage without the key?

He popped another cookie into his mouth and chewed, grinning.

Answer: you cut the wire.

You get a strong pair of wire cutters.

Snip, snip.

It would take only a few minutes to cut a hole big enough for Benny to slip through.

He headed for the house. Harold knew exactly where to put his hands on the wire cutters.

It wouldn't even be stealing. He'd "borrow" the cutters and return them on Monday. No one would miss them over the weekend.

He emptied his backpack to make room. He grabbed a few more cookies from the kitchen and checked the clock. Three forty-five. School was over, but Mr. Gunter always stayed late on Fridays to clean up.

A few minutes later Harold was creeping around the back of the school. He stayed close to the building, trying to look casual and invisible at the same time. He had to be the only kid in the world who'd ever sneaked into school on a Friday afternoon!

The outside door of the industrial arts room was open for fresh air. A wedge of wood held it ajar. Harold prayed that Mr. Gunter was sitting in the teachers' lounge sipping coffee.

His shadow preceded him into the room like a black ghost. "Harold, what can we do for you?" Mr. Gunter wasn't in the teachers' lounge sipping coffee. He was standing in front of Harold, blocking his way.

Big and gentle, Mr. Gunter was everyone's favorite teacher. The curly hair on his forearms was golden with sawdust. The stuff clung to his work pants like pollen on a bee's legs.

"I already got my helpers for today," he said, gesturing toward two boys on the other side of the room. One was Jake Gunter, a tall eighth grader and Mr. G's nephew. The other helper was Todd Sims. Todd looked embarrassed and went back to his sweeping. Harold felt too panicked to care.

He hadn't planned on a crowd. He had pictured an empty room, a quick grab, and a fast getaway. His mouth went dry and his brain whispered Abandon ship! But his feet felt embedded in cement.

"I need to borrow some wire cutters. It's an emergency. My mother got her hand caught in the wire on our dog pen." The lies flowed like lava while Harold's face burned volcano hot. Gunter would never believe him in a trillion years.

"My gosh, Harold, sure!" Mr. Gunter's kind face showed concern. He believed him! Harold felt like crawling under a rock.

"Jakey, get those cutters, will you? The big ones." Jake walked toward the wall where about a hundred tools were hanging, each in its special place, outlined in black paint. If a tool didn't get put away at the end of a shop period, anyone could tell exactly where it belonged. All you had to do was find its silhouette on the wall.

Mr. Gunter handed the tool over to Harold. "I'll have Jakey walk home with you," he said, "so you won't have to bring these back."

Harold's hands shook as he unzipped his backpack and slipped the wire cutters inside. He didn't want anyone coming home with him. And he couldn't return these things today.

"Um, it's okay, Mr. G. I live right near here," Harold said, trying to avoid looking over at Todd. "But I don't think I'll have time to bring the wire cutters back today."

"No problem, Harold." Mr. Gunter walked him toward the door. "Monday'll be fine. I hope your mom's okay."

Harold caught a glimpse of Todd over Mr. G's shoulder. He was staring at Harold with absolutely no expression on his face. Harold mumbled his thanks and bolted outside.

He felt a little sick. He was used to telling white lies, not huge black ones. These had left a lousy taste in his mouth.

But he had the cutters. Benny was practically a free chimpanzee.

He decided to treat himself to some M&M's at Ryan's Pharmacy. He was trying to decide between plain or the kind with peanuts inside when he felt something nudge his elbow. It was Todd Sims, and he was grinning.

Harold felt his face begin to burn. He stared at the candy rack without seeing a thing.

"Gee, your poor mom. Stuck in a fence while you rush home to help her."

Harold couldn't think of a thing to say. The temperature in Ryan's shot up about fifty degrees.

"I don't know how Gunter believed your story," Todd said, scanning the candy selections. "I sure don't."

Harold didn't know where to look. Old Mr. Ryan hawk-eyed the boys from his stool behind the prescription counter. Harold felt trapped.

"I confess," he whispered. "I'm robbing a bank."

"With wire cutters? Neat, Pinto." Todd picked out a Mounds bar and paid Mr. Ryan.

Harold had lost his appetite for candy and he put the M&M's back. The wire cutters clunked against his back as he moved toward the door. Mr. Ryan's eyes followed him, trying to see how many candy bars Harold had slipped inside that pack.

Outside, Todd held out his Mounds in front of Harold's face. "Want a bite?"

Harold shook his head. He shifted the pack to a more comfortable position on his shoulders. "Look," he said, inspecting the ground between his feet and Todd's, "I'm sorry about what I said last week. I . . . I'm glad you liked my report."

Todd took a big bite of his candy. He mumbled something about its being no problem.

Apologizing was a new experience for Harold. He hadn't known he was going to say anything, it just came out. But now he had to get home. He had a lot of planning to do. "See you Monday," he said to Todd. "I gotta go."

Todd looked him square in the eyes. "To rescue your mother?"

"Yeah," Harold answered. He started walking toward home, and Todd kept up. Todd knew he was full of it, Harold told himself. But he wasn't telling anyone about Benny. This time no one would laugh at him.

"Know what the guys say about you?" Todd was a full head taller than Harold. And he wasn't as klutzy as the rest of the kids they knew. He sort of glided as he walked.

"I don't want to hear it."

Todd went right on. "They say you'd have a few friends if you'd lighten up."

"I don't need any friends," Harold said, which was a lie. He figured Todd wasn't fooled, just the way Mr. Stanley wasn't fooled.

"That's what I mean," Todd said. "A guy tries to—"

"Drop it, okay?" Harold felt himself getting mad. Not exactly at Todd, more at himself. He liked having somebody to talk to, but he didn't want Todd—or anyone else—butting into his business.

They walked for quite a while without saying anything. Todd started singing in a loud, smooth voice ". . . and my hearrrt is a vi-o-liinnn!"

Harold wondered why Todd didn't get mad. No matter what he said to him, the guy never got ticked off. And I'm always ripped, Harold admitted to himself. He kicked a Pepsi can someone had tossed out of a car window.

Todd intercepted the can with his foot and passed it back to Harold. They shot it back and forth like that, nice and easy, without talking until they were in front of Harold's house.

"This is where I live." The house looked pretty shabby in the late afternoon sun. Harold wished he'd taken the time to rake the lawn after he mowed it. "I gotta go in," he said.

Todd leaned on a fire hydrant and passed the Pepsi can from foot to foot. He nodded at Harold's backpack. "So what's the story on the wire cutters?" Then he smiled, squinting into the sun. "You can trust me, Pinto."

Just then the Subaru whipped into the driveway. Harold's mother tooted the horn, then climbed out. She waved and started hustling groceries out of the rear compartment. "I could use four more hands, you guys."

Harold watched a robin mangling a night crawler on the grass. He felt a little embarrassed that his lie to Gunter was now a proven fact. He didn't want Todd to think he went around lying to everyone.

"Okay," he said quietly. "But if you say anything at school you're dead."

Harold started walking toward the car. Todd followed him. "I'm kidnapping a chimpanzee," Harold said.

Nine

"YOU'RE *what?*"

"Shut up, okay?" Harold headed for the house with Todd right behind him. They each carried a large bag of food. Harold's mother was tearing around the kitchen.

"Thanks, boys, you're a big help." She looked at Todd and smiled. "Do I know you?"

"I'm Todd Sims. My mother and I just moved here a couple months ago." Todd set his bag on the counter.

"From New York City."

"How do you like our little village?" Harold mother asked. "Watertown must seem very different to you."

"It is. I miss my friends, but I really like being in the country."

Harold watched his mother and Todd chatting away as if they were old buddies. Why couldn't he be like that? He always clammed up. Todd seemed really at ease, and he'd just met Harold's mother a few seconds ago!

She suddenly raced out of the kitchen, talking over her shoulder. "I have to be at the club in six minutes! Harold, would you please put the food away? And that casserole goes in the oven at five fifteen." Her voice now came from the stairs leading up to her room. "Nice meeting you, Todd!"

Harold set the grocery bag on the counter next to Todd's. He slid his backpack onto the floor, hoping his mother hadn't noticed its odd shape. He began unpacking the bags. Todd helped, putting obvious things like milk and juice into the refrigerator. "You're kidnapping a *monkey?*" he whispered.

"It's a chimpanzee," Harold said quietly. "And I'm not really kidnapping him, just giving him his freedom." He began dividing the groceries into separate piles for cupboards, freezer, refrigerator.

"You lost me Pinto. First you—"

"Don't call me Pinto, okay? It's Harold. *H–A—*"

"Okay, okay. So where is this chimpanzee?" Todd moved a carton of eggs and a head of lettuce to the refrigerator.

"At a lab on the other side of town." Harold balanced a stack of frozen vegetables in both hands and opened the freezer door with his foot. He dumped the cartons in and bumped the door shut with one knee. "I've been visiting him. They're gonna kill him if I don't let him loose."

Todd shook his head in wonder. "Just like that? You're just gonna walk in and spring this mon—chimpanzee?"

63

Todd's voice took on an ironic tone. "Isn't there some little law against that sort of thing?"

"Benny's been in cages his whole life. It isn't fair, and I plan to do something about it." Harold liked the way he said that. He sounded as if he fought society all the time. He hoped Todd got the impression that he felt pretty confident, even though he didn't.

Harold grabbed his pack off the floor and pulled out the wire cutters. "Think these will work?"

"Can I ask one question?" Todd ran his fingers gently over the business end of the cutters. "What happens after you let this Benjy loose?"

"Benny."

"Whatever. Chimpanzees don't live in New York, you know."

Harold slipped the wire cutters back into his pack and put the last of the canned goods into a cupboard. "They don't live in cages, either," he said. "At least when he's loose, he'll have trees to climb and fresh air."

"And barbed-wire fences to get caught on, and dogs to chase him and trucks to run him over." Todd flattened an empty bag and handed it to Harold. "And what happens when it snows?"

Harold added the bags to the ones his mother kept squished between the stove and the refrigerator. He wished Todd wouldn't ask so many questions. Why hadn't *he* thought of all the dangers Benny would face once he was free? He was safer where he was, in his cage inside the brick building, Harold had to admit. But, he asked himself, was Benny happy there?

"Winter is six months away," he said finally. Which didn't answer Todd's questions, but it was the best he could come up with.

There was a pause in the conversation, a long one. This had all seemed so simple an hour ago. Now, with all Sims's dumb questions, Harold found himself totally confused. And he knew the questions weren't dumb, either. Truth was, he hadn't thought this plan through. And it ticked him off that suddenly his great idea didn't seem so great anymore.

"Know what I think?" Todd was great at answering his own questions. "I think this chimp, if you *do* let him out, will die. Or"—here Todd used his forefinger for emphasis the way Mr. Stanley sometimes did—"he'll go berserk and end up hurting some little kid somewhere."

Harold thought of the old guy at LAPS and his stumpy finger. If a chimp could bite off a finger when he was *in* a cage, what could he do on the outside? Was Benny just friendly to Harold because of all the food he'd brought him? Harold felt himself getting a headache. He wished he'd never told Sims his plan.

Harold's mother breezed back into the kitchen. She was dressed for golf: all pale yellow with a light green sweater draped around her shoulders. She smelled like a bunch of flowers. "Oh, great, you've put everything away." She touched Harold lightly on the shoulder on her way to the breezeway. "I'll be back at six. You won't forget the casserole?"

Harold heard the Subaru start up. His mother's perfume smell gradually faded along with the sound of the car. But

Todd's words rang out loud and clear in his head. "He'll . . . end up hurting some little kid somewhere." Harold kicked at a grocery receipt that had fallen out of one of the bags.

Todd was staring at him. "You really must like animals a lot."

Harold nodded. "Yeah. They're better than people most of the time."

"I don't know," Todd said. "Some of us are okay." He smiled. "I had a lot of neat friends back in the City. We did fun stuff together. Movies, ball games in Central Park, parties, everything. The guys here are out of it." He ran a fingernail down the screen on the breezeway door.

"Some of us are okay," Harold said, trying to imitate Todd's tone.

Todd laughed. "Yeah, but the only guy who isn't a total jerk turns out to be a monkey thief." Todd held up both hands. "Sorry, chimpanzee thief."

Harold locked his eyes on the casserole dish. He wondered whether it was tuna or chicken. He also wondered if he could really go through with his escape plan for Benny. Maybe *he* was one of the total jerks.

Todd glanced at the kitchen clock. "I gotta go," he said. He held the screen door open with the toe of one sneaker.

"You want to help me do it? Let Benny out?" Harold hadn't known he was going to ask. His words surprised him as much as they seemed to surprise Todd. Lately, Harold realized he didn't seem to have much control over what he said.

Todd drew his toe back into the kitchen. "You're really gonna do it? He'll probably die, you know."

66

Harold nodded. He did know. But what he wasn't sure of was whether it was kinder to let him die slowly in his cage. If Benny had a choice, which would he choose? Harold asked himself one more time. "I think he'd rather be free," he said, finally, hoping he sounded sure of himself. "No matter what."

"And you're goin' in there with your wire cutters and let him go, just like that. Aren't there any guards?"

"There's one old guy, but he doesn't come around a lot. And a few scientists, but they stay in another building." Was it lying not to tell Todd the old guy had already caught him once? And that the girl, Carrie, had told him the place was private to snoopers? "It'll work," he said. "I've been there lots of times."

Todd shook his head and let out a long sigh. "I gotta think about this," he told Harold. "When were you thinking about doing it?"

Harold knew if he waited too long he'd chicken out.

"Tomorrow," he said.

"No can do. I have a . . . I have classes. What about Sunday?"

Did this mean Sims had made up his mind? Sunday was only two days away. He didn't even have a plan, for cripe's sake. But he would, and whatever he came up with would work better with two people. "Okay, Sunday. Let's meet here about ten."

Todd was out the door. "You better have this all worked out," he said through the screen. "And make it ten thirty. I practice two hours in the morning."

Harold leaned on the doorjamb. "Practice what?"

"Dunk shots," Todd said with a serious look on his face. "What else?"

Harold watched Sims leap over a fire hydrant and take off down Clancy Street. He felt better knowing he'd confided in someone, even if that someone refused to help. Harold sighed and looked at the clock. It was a little after four thirty. He carried his pack with the wire cutters into his bedroom and hid it under a pile of clothes on the bottom of his closet.

What a mess. The room looked pretty junky. He'd have to do something about it one of these days. He tapped on the aquarium side. Tammy and Willie responded with squeaks and mad dashing around their cage.

Harold wondered if these gerbils hated living in the aquarium. Was he making them prisoners? Could he accuse the LAPS scientists of something he was guilty of himself? Shouldn't he let his pets have their freedom as he planned to do for Benny? How long would a gerbil last scampering around the neighborhood?

He transferred some clothes to a chair and flopped down on his bed. Todd was right. There were too many questions without answers, some he hadn't even asked himself till now. Like, would Benny just sit there like a good chimp while Harold cut a hole in his cage? What would they do if anyone caught them, wire cutters in hand? How would they get Benny out the window of his building?

He rolled over and gave his pillow a punch. His glasses bit into his cheek so he took them off. One big question continued to nag like a toothache. What was really kinder to Benny: letting the scientists put him to death or giving him a chance as a free chimpanzee?

Harold stared at the wall. He wished he knew what *Benny* wanted. He wished chimpanzees could talk. He wished a lot of things.

Ten

"HAROLD? Where are you? Did you put the casserole . . . why isn't the oven on? Harold?"

He jumped up, still half asleep when she opened his door. "Oh, Harold. You said you'd start dinner! Now it'll take another half hour."

He swung his feet to the floor, groggy from his nap. He scratched his head, found his glasses on the bed and headed for the kitchen. His mother followed him down the hall, talking loud enough to be heard over the soft thuds of her rubber spikes.

"I have a million things to do before tomorrow morning." She stood watching as Harold turned the oven dial to 400 degrees. She looked about a thousand miles away.

"You're going to be rid of me this weekend," she said. She lifted one edge of the tinfoil covering the yellow casserole dish and poked a finger into its contents. The dish used to have a cover, but it got broken about a year ago, around the time Harold's father moved out. "I'm going to Syracuse with Mavis and Cora. We signed up for a golf workshop."

She sounded excited, not sorry like some mothers would have been to leave their kid alone for a weekend. Harold took dishes and glasses from the cupboards, silver from a drawer. He wiped the table with a sponge. Why was his mother just standing there watching him?

"Trudy Ford is giving the lessons. *The* Trudy Ford," she added, placing a palm on the stove top. "Why does this thing take forever to heat up?"

Who the heck is Trudy Ford? He didn't ask.

His mother snapped her fingers. "I have to call Mrs. Kinney to stay with you!" She hurried out of the kitchen. "Throw that in the oven now, will you?"

He felt like throwing it out the window. She didn't even ask what *his* plans were. Wasn't it possible that he might have liked to go to Syracuse? He wouldn't, of course. But still, she could have asked.

He opened the oven, then stepped back as the heat blasted him in the face. He slid the casserole onto the rack and closed the door.

Mrs. Kinney was a good sitter. Meaning she was no problem to Harold. She was around fifty years old with all her chicks out of the nest, as she put it. She was always into some new project. One time it was knot tying. She'd bought herself an old Boy Scout manual and taught herself every knot in the book. Another time she'd showed up with four lemons and a book called *Juggling for Everyone*. Harold could still hear those lemons bouncing off the floor.

Mrs. Kinney always let Harold "fish for himself." Another of her expressions. He didn't mind. He had experience fishing for himself.

He leaned on the sink and stared out the window as the casserole did its thing. He could feel the kitchen begin to warm up even through the oven door. Why were they having a casserole on such a warm day?

He wondered if Todd would really show up on Sunday morning. Should he call and remind him? He didn't even know where Todd Sims lived. In fact, Harold realized, he didn't know anything about him.

But he liked him and thought that Todd felt the same way. He wasn't sure why. He sure hadn't been too nice the first couple of times Todd spoke to him. But that was behind him. People are allowed to make mistakes, aren't they?

It felt good having a new friend. Well, Todd wasn't exactly a friend yet. But he might be one day.

Good smells were beginning to float around the kitchen. Harold set the table. How many times had he placed the same white dishes on these faded place mats? Or folded paper napkins and put them to the left of the plates? Now he did it without thinking about what went where.

An old picture clicked into his brain. He was real little, around three or four. Messing around on the kitchen floor with his miniature cars. His mom and dad were talking, joking around, getting dinner ready.

He remembered their feet and legs brushing past him, never stepping on his fingers or the cars. Once in a while his dad would grab him and swing him up to the ceiling. Harold had squealed, loving every second of it.

That sudden swoop into the air, and his father's strong hands holding him under the arms still gave Harold a funny feeling in his stomach. Even after all these years, if he closed his eyes, he could see his father's face exactly the way it looked then.

His stomach growled. He added salt and pepper to the table and a mug for his mother's coffee. She drank regular at the bank, but at night she wanted decaffeinated. Harold wondered how they got the caffeine out.

His mother hurried in, wearing her white terrycloth robe with the floppy hood. She never used the hood except to dry her hair, which is what she was doing with it now.

Harold smelled a mixture of baby powder and some kind of sweet shampoo. She looked a lot more relaxed than she had a half hour ago. Harold watched, without letting her see him, while she dried her hair with the hood of her robe. When he was little, she'd grab him and tickle his face with her wet hair.

Harold ripped a half head of Boston lettuce into small chunks. Tear your lettuce, don't cut it, he'd read somewhere. What's the difference? He found a hunk of cucumber, a tomato, and a few wrinkled mushrooms. There were plenty of onions he could have sliced, but he didn't feel like crying. His mother might think it was because she was going away.

He chopped the vegetables and tossed them into a big bowl. They both liked the same dressing, some green stuff with about a million spices and herbs floating around in it.

73

Harold liked to shake the bottle and pretend the herbs were snowflakes. He poured himself some milk and sat down opposite his mother.

"Do you mind that I'm going away? You're awfully serious tonight." She let the hood fall to her shoulders and shook her hair the way Max used to. "I didn't give you much notice, did I. But you like Mrs. Kinney."

Harold speared a cucumber slice with his fork. Would it matter if he did mind? "How're you getting to Syracuse?" he asked.

"Mavis is driving. I don't trust the Subaru any farther than the bank anymore. First it was that *ping-ping*ing. Now it's a kind of rumble." She glanced at Harold. "I wish you'd take up mechanics at school and save me a fortune on car bills."

Harold shrugged and straightened his silverware. He didn't want to learn about fixing cars any more than she did.

His mother leaned over and cracked open the oven door. Harold heard the bubbling noise and felt another rush of hot air.

She stood and cinched the belt of her robe tighter, then took two potholders from a drawer and brought the sizzling dish to the table. "Quick, put something underneath!"

Harold jumped up and found a trivet shaped like a fish in the drawer where they kept all the stuff that didn't fit anywhere else. His mother set the casserole down and removed the tinfoil with her fork. Steam and the smell of hot cheese and tuna fish rose into the air over the table.

Harold's mouth began to water, even though he wasn't especially hungry. He thought he saw a few green things poking out of the noodles and cheese. Peas? Broccoli? "When's Mrs. Kinney coming?" he asked.

"Mavis and Cora will be here around eight thirty. Mrs. K will get here just after, she says." Harold's mother spooned a steaming mound of Tuna Surprise onto his plate. She dropped a thimbleful on her own, then loaded up with salad.

They ate. Harold burned his mouth on a chunk of boiling tuna fish. He gulped his milk and immediately started choking.

"Are you okay?" His mother reached across the table and gave him a few brisk whacks on the back.

Between the hot tuna and the milk and his mother's back slaps, Harold could hardly breathe. His eyes filled with tears. When he tried to take in a deep breath, he started coughing. He thought he might throw up.

Somehow his mother was behind him. He felt himself being lifted out of his chair. Her arms circled his chest, just below his ribs. "Harold, let yourself go limp!" he heard her cry. "I've got you, just relax!"

He did. She gave a few quick squeezes. He tasted the tuna fish that had been forced up his throat into his mouth. He could breathe again, but the tears kept slipping down his face.

His mother set him gently back into his chair. He felt like a little kid again. He hadn't felt her arms around him for about ten years, it seemed.

She set a glass of water in front of him. "You scared the

life out of me!'' she said. "Are you okay now?''

Harold wiped his face with his napkin. He took a deep breath and nodded. When he looked up, his mother's face was almost the color of her robe. "Where'd you learn how to do that?'' he asked.

She smiled. "I know a lot of things I've never told you.''

Harold started eating again. He took his time. He had been tricked into talking to her, he realized. But it's hard to stay mad at someone who stops you from choking to death.

Eleven

HAROLD WOKE UP suddenly in the middle of the night. His feet were tangled in the sheet. His heart raced as he lay in the dark. There were tears in his eyes.

It's not real, he told himself over and over. In his nightmare, Benny was slowly sinking into a pit of quicksand. Harold had stretched a tree branch toward him, but it was too short. Benny sank, screaming and waving his arms.

Harold shivered. He freed his legs and pulled the covers up around his neck. He saw Benny's eyes as clearly as if he were with Harold in his bedroom.

His mother shook his shoulder at eight twenty the next morning, Saturday. "Harold? Mavis and Cora will be here in a few minutes. I'd like you up before I leave."

He watched his mother checking out the mess in his room. She picked a shirt off the floor, smelled it, then hung it in his closet. She bent for a pair of jeans, then straightened up again. "Why am I doing this?" she said out loud.

She wore a new, pale blue outfit. Her white golf shoes looked freshly polished. Her perfume smelled like violets.

"Harold? Five minutes, please?" She waited till Harold grunted, then went out. From the kitchen he heard dishes and things being moved around. Coffee smells began to blot out the perfume.

He stretched, yawned long and loud, then kicked off the covers. He remembered his nightmare. Now, with sunlight pouring into his room, the awful scene was less vivid. But Harold didn't need a dream expert to figure it out. Benny was going to die.

If he remained in his cage, he'd be put to death by the LAPS people. If Harold let him out, he'd be free for a while, then starve or freeze to death this winter. But at least that way he'd die as a normal chimpanzee, not as a prisoner.

He dressed quickly. His hands shook as he tied his sneaker laces, and this was only Saturday. What would he be like tomorrow?

He lifted Tammy out of the aquarium and let her snuggle up against his stomach. The way he figured it, Benny's life was in his hands as surely as this gerbil's was. He could leave Benny alone and let the scientists put him to sleep. Or he could use those wire cutters hidden in the bottom of his closet.

Tammy crawled up his chest and tried to wriggle down

the front of his T-shirt. "What should I do?" he asked her, rubbing his face against her furry little body.

She squeaked like mad when Harold dropped her into the pine chips. He filled the food dish and replaced the screen top.

In the kitchen, he sat sipping orange juice and watched his mother move around the room. She checked the contents of the refrigerator about six times. She scribbled a note to Mrs. Kinney. She made Harold study the phone number of the Syracuse Hotel that she'd written on the phone pad.

"I'll be back tomorrow around suppertime," she told him, tipping the last of her coffee into the sink. She glared at the clock. "Where *are* they?"

Her blue overnight bag was parked by the door, next to her clubs. The bags matched each other, and her outfit. All she needed now were blue golf balls.

A horn sounded out front. Harold's mother grabbed her bag and slung the golf clubs over a shoulder. She stood by the door and looked at Harold until he began to feel uncomfortable. "Will you be all right until Mrs. Kinney gets here?"

"Mom, I'm thirteen, remember?" He wanted her to stay home, but he didn't know why. But he also wanted her out of the house. He wondered if he should offer to carry her clubs outside.

Before he could decide, she bumped the screen door open with one hip. "Well, I'll see you then." She gave him another look, shaking her head and smiling. "Your hair!"

In a second she was gone.

He heard the women's excited voices shattering the morning stillness, car doors opening and closing, then Mavis's car roaring away up Clancy Street. Harold sat where he was, thinking about the three friends off for a weekend, laughing, having a good time. He'd never felt lonelier.

While he was pouring milk over his Cheerios, Mrs. Kinney knocked lightly on the breezeway door. He hadn't even heard her car drive up.

It had been about two months since she'd been here. Either she'd shrunk or Harold had grown. He could look her in the eyes now, almost.

She flashed Harold a warm smile and tapped him on the shoulder. "Does Mama keep the tea bags in the same place?" She dropped her carryall near the door and gave Harold a long, appraising look. Then she nodded as if he'd passed inspection. "Why am I babysitting for a young man?" she asked, but he knew she was half teasing.

Mrs. Kinney was a short, pudgy woman. Harold thought she was pretty frisky for her age. Today she wore a yellow dress with white ankle socks and those black Chinese shoes that a lot of the girls at school were wearing now.

Her eyes flitted around like restless blue moths. Her hands never seemed to rest. They touched things, straightened things, patted things.

Harold wondered what she'd brought to keep those hands busy this time. Pointing with his spoon he said, "The mugs are next to the cookbooks now."

He ate his cereal while she fixed her tea, glanced in the

refrigerator, read his mother's note. "Golf lessons?"

Harold nodded. "In Syracuse."

She smiled, then floated to a chair at the table. "I hate athletic people!" Harold knew she was kidding again. He didn't think Mrs. K hated anyone.

"Do you mind being left alone with an old lady?"

Harold shook his head. But he wondered why he couldn't tell her what was really in his mind. Yeah, I mind a lot. But kids don't make rules. Grown-ups do.

"Any plans for the weekend?" Her eyes fluttered over his face. What is she looking for? he wondered.

He looked down at the soggy Cheerios left in his bowl. He felt like shocking her with the news that he and a friend were planning to break a chimpanzee out of his cage. He fought the urge.

"It's a secret," he said instead. He rinsed his glass and bowl and left them in the sink.

"I love secrets," Mrs. Kinney said, sounding around ten years old. "How about a little hint?"

Harold smiled and shook his head. He didn't feel so lonely now. "I'll be in my room for a while," he said.

"And I'll be here if you need me." Mrs. Kinney waggled a few fingers at him.

Harold padded down the hall. He pulled a notebook out from under his mattress and sat at his desk. He read over last night's words.

The list covered one whole page. Writing this stuff down made Harold realize that he wasn't cut out for breaking and entering. Maybe this was why he'd had that nightmare.

WHAT I KNOW

1. Benny should be free.
2. He's usually alone except for morning feeding.
3. He likes me.
4. He likes fruit and M&M's.
5. He bit the old guy's finger off—he says!

WHAT I DON'T KNOW

1. Who's around LAPS on Sundays?
2. How long will it take to cut the wires?
3. Are the wire cutters stong enough?
4. Will Benny start howling when he sees Todd?
5. How will we get him out of the cage? Out of the building?
6. What if he attacks us?
7. Should we just let him wander off into the woods?
8. What will happen if we get caught?
9. Is Benny dangerous?
10. Will Todd show up tomorrow?

He scribbled in his notebook for half the morning, throwing away more pages than he kept. He thought of more questions, but didn't write them down. His simple plan was getting out of control.

Maybe he should just give it up. Was he trying to play God? If only he hadn't met Benny, he wouldn't have this problem. No, Harold argued with himself, Benny has the problem. Was I somehow sent to him? Am *I* the key to his cage?

And what about the rest of the chimps at the lab? How many were locked up in that other building? Were they doomed as soon as they outlived their usefulness? Was Benny's little private building really death row for chimps?

He knew from his reading that over 300,000 laboratory animals are killed every day in the United States alone. Mice, rats, dogs, cats, guinea pigs, rabbits, insects. And chimpanzees.

He'd been shocked when he read that. Some of the animals die as a result of the experiments performed on them. Others are put to death on purpose, usually with an overdose of some anesthetic. He wondered when Benny was scheduled for his overdose.

Harold dug his hands into his hair. He studied the page in front of him. He drew circles around question 5 in the What I Don't Know column. How *would* he get Benny outside after they cut a hole in his cage? After he figured that out, the rest of his questions would take care of themselves, one way or another.

He circled question 9. *Is* Benny dangerous? Does he think of me as his friend? Do chimpanzees think about anything?

Harold threw down his Magic Marker. This was giving him a headache. He closed his eyes and tried to picture the room and the row of cages. Benny's cage sat about ten feet from the window. It might as well have been a thousand feet. The door was closer, but anyone looking out a window in the big building could see that door easily.

Benny would have to go through the window, as Harold had. But how? Would he just hop out? Would he be willing to leave his cage? Harold had read how a lot of caged animals seemed to like their prisons.

If only the cages were closer to that window. Harold sat straight up in his chair. Of course! They were on wheels. He and Todd could roll all three cages right up to the window!

He threw himself on his bed and grinned at the ceiling. It would work. All of it. He'd pile some fruit on the window ledge. Once the hole was cut, he and Todd would just move the cages so Benny was sitting smack in front of the open window. Would he stay or go?

Harold thought Benny would go for it. Chimpanzees were intelligent, right? He'd know for sure in twenty-four hours.

Twelve

ON SUNDAY MORNING Todd showed up at ten thirty. He was wearing army camouflage pants with about ten zippered pockets and a dark green M*A*S*H T-shirt.

Harold was impressed. Sims would blend in with the trees. His own black jeans and T-shirt made him look like a cat burglar.

He led Todd through the living room where Mrs. Kinney sat on the floor, leaning against the sofa. She'd placed a mug of tea and a plate of orange sections near her elbow on a little table. Soft music floated from the radio.

Half a dozen small paper animals stood or sat around Mrs. Kinney's feet. She had folded colored paper into fish, birds, dogs, even a giraffe. A half-finished butterfly rested on her lap.

Harold picked up a dog. "What kind is he?"

"A dachshund," Mrs. Kinney said, "one of those hot-dog dogs." She peered up at Todd and smiled. "Hello, I'm Ida Kinney."

Todd shook her hand. "Todd Sims. I really like your Origami. We did it in art last year."

Mrs. Kinney beamed. "What can you make?"

Todd blushed. "Wrinkled paper, mostly. I didn't get too good at it."

"It takes a lot of practice." She looked at Harold, still turning the little brown dog over in his fingers. "Maybe I'll give you boys a lesson later. How about it?"

"Great!" Todd said.

Harold sat the dachshund back on the floor and tugged lightly on Todd's arm. Mrs. Kinney waved and picked up the paper butterfly as the boys walked down the hall.

Todd squatted down in front of the aquarium. He made little clicking noises with his tongue. Tammy and Willie sat up, but they seemed to know he wasn't Harold.

Todd turned around and did a quick little dance step. "Guess what I am."

Harold looked at him with one eye closed. "Fidel Castro." He fished the backpack out from under his bed.

Todd shook his head. "But you're close. I'm a guerrilla. Get it? *Guerrilla?*"

Harold smiled at the pun. He stuck his arms through the straps and shrugged the pack into a comfortable position. Along with the wire cutters, which weighed about ten pounds, he'd loaded up with bananas, apples, and two grapefruits. His mother would flip when she found the fridge burglarized. Maybe she'd think Mrs. Kinney had gone on a fruit binge.

86

"Nice room." Todd looked around, checking out the animal posters covering the walls.

Harold felt good about the way his room looked. Knowing Todd was coming, he'd spent the morning cleaning up. His bed had clean sheets, and the cover was flat and tucked in. He'd hit the closet, too, organizing his stuff and throwing out about five years of old magazines. He wondered if his mother would notice the difference.

"Let's go." He slung his earphones around his neck and clipped the cassette player to his belt. He pawed through a drawer until he found his jackknife.

"When do I get to hear the big plan?" Todd asked."I'll explain everything when we get there." Harold left his room. The weight of the pack against his back made him feel grown-up, under control. But he noticed that he kept wiping his hands on his jeans.

"You're sure this is gonna work, right?"

Harold nodded. "It'll work fine." It has to work, he said to himself.

"So where is this place, anyway?" Todd followed Harold through the garage, then outside. Harold waited while Todd retrieved his bike from where he'd stashed it behind the house. "You got a dog?" Todd asked, noticing Max's pen.

"Had one. He died." Harold climbed on his bike. "The lab is on Turnback Road, a few miles from here." He led the way. The heavy pack bumped against his back every time he went over a crack.

Todd started right in singing at the top of his lungs. Harold didn't understand the song Todd never seemed to grow tired of. How could a heart be a violin?

He took one hand off the handlebars and slid his ear-phones into place. He pushed the play button and turned up the volume until Willie Nelson drowned out Todd Sims

He soon wished he'd worn shorts. The day was sticky, and it wasn't even noon yet. The sun shone out of a sky so blue it looked fake.

What am I doing? he asked himself for the hundredth time. He swallowed to get rid of the pukey feeling in his stomach. This is nuts. I could go to jail. At the very least his mother would ground him for a million years if she found out.

He forced his mind to focus on Benny. He was doing this for the chimp. No animal should be locked in a cage against his will.

He chose side streets with broad trees that blocked out the sun. People were out doing weekend things—washing cars, planting bright clumps of flowers; kids were whipping down driveways on skateboards.

Todd pulled up next to Harold and tapped him on the shoulder.

"Turnback is at the end of this street," Harold said. "Go right!"

Todd flashed a thumbs up and took off, hunched over his handlebars. Harold tried to do the same, but the pack threw him off balance.

The next time he saw Todd he was sprawled on the grass under the LAPS sign. Chewing on a blade of grass. Not even out of breath.

Harold showed him where to hide his bike. Todd carried the pack as they started into the woods. "Whaddaya got in here, anyway?"

88

"Food for Benny." Harold concentrated on walking quietly over the dry leaves and pine needles, but he made noise anyway. Todd moved as soundlessly as a deer. Was there anything he couldn't do?

Todd tugged on the pack straps. "What's he eat, rocks? This thing weighs a ton!"

Harold told him what he'd put in the pack.

"Fruit!" Todd laughed. "Where's he gonna get fruit after he's loose?"

Todd had a point. Watertown was located ten miles from the southern shore of Lake Ontario. It wasn't exactly known for oranges and bananas. Plenty of apples, but not till around September. If Benny is still alive in September, Harold reminded himself.

But there were other things out here a chimp could eat: birds' eggs, leaves and grass, berries, a few kinds of nuts. If he could survive over twenty years of scientific experiments, Harold figured, he might make it in the New York woods.

He was more concerned about the harsh winters they got up here. Over four feet of snow last year. He remembered Todd's comments. What *would* Benny do when it snowed? Did chimpanzees hibernate like bears?

It didn't matter, Harold told himself once more. Benny would be happier free. Anything had to be better than living in a cage. Harold kept that thought in the front of his mind as he led the way toward the LAPS buildings.

He pointed through the trees. The back of Benny's little house was just visible. They watched and listened for over five minutes. Then Harold sat in the pine needles and explained his plan to Todd.

89

Todd made him repeat a lot of things, like the part about rolling the cages over to the window. And he asked a lot of questions. How long would the whole thing take? Was this chimpanzee nice and friendly? Was Harold *sure* someone wouldn't show up with Benny's noon meal?

Harold answered every question. It felt good to know that Todd took him and Benny seriously. Besides, he needed, no, *he wanted* Todd's help. Also, the longer they sat chatting, the longer Harold could put off crawling through that window with the wire cutters.

"This is like stealing, you know." Todd pitched a small pinecone at Harold's knee. "We could get in big trouble."

"I know. But what about Benny, and all those other chimps? *Someone* has to do something." He chucked the cone back toward Todd. "They're gonna kill him."

"Yeah, I know." Todd nodded, slowly. "I know. It's not fair. It rots."

Harold told Todd about Carrie and the old man with the bitten-off finger and about his numerous visits to Benny during the past week.

"You're really into this, aren't you?" Todd said.

Harold watched a patch of sunlight grow slowly larger as the clouds moved. Brown pine needles turned to gold as the sun's light fell on them. He looked up. Todd was watching him.

" Get this," Harold said. "You know how everyone's always telling us smoking's no good for our health? Causes lung cancer, stunts our growth?" He checked to make sure he had Todd's attention.

"Well, there's this lab somewhere in Texas that uses

baboons as guinea pigs. No, I'm serious. They put the baboons in these harness things and make them smoke hundreds of cigarettes a week. Maybe thousands. Then they take X-rays of the baboons' lungs. They cut open their hearts and veins."

Harold stopped, trying to picture what he'd just said. He looked at Todd. "What do you think they find?"

Todd didn't answer. His eyes were intent on Harold's face.

"Lung cancer. Hardening of the arteries. The same stuff people get from smoking too much." Harold raised his voice. "And it's the scientists that *give* the baboons that stuff!"

He stopped again, searching for the right words, feeling that he had to convince Todd. "It's like the scientists believe humans are more important than the animals they use for experiments. But why should we be? Who invented nuclear bombs, people or animals? Who pollutes the rivers and starts wars and—"

"Hold it." Todd sat up straight. "If scientists don't use animals, how are they supposed to experiment? On trees?"

"On us." Harold had been thinking about this since he started writing his report weeks ago. Why not use real humans in experiments instead of animals that resemble humans?

"I bet a lot of people would let themselves be used in experiments if they got paid," Harold said. "Like people who are sick and know they're gonna die pretty soon. Maybe they'd feel proud to do something with their bodies to help other people."

"Like donating your body to science before you die?"

"Yeah. Only the scientists would have to get your permission first. Nobody asked Benny if they could lock him up for twenty years." Harold turned and looked through the trees at the brick building. "They just did it."

Todd shook his head. "You're amazing. Last week the guys were calling you the chimpanzee kid. They told me you'd forget about the chimps the same way you did the seals. I bet 'em they were wrong."

Harold felt himself blush. "Why?"

"Just a hunch."

Harold stood up and grabbed the pack. "You ready?" he asked.

Thirteen

THROUGH THE OPEN WINDOW, Harold heard Benny's soft little grunts. He also heard a man's voice, talking low. "Someone's in there!" he whispered.

Todd put his mouth close to Harold's ear. "Who?"

Harold shook his head. He hoped it was someone feeding Benny, not doing something else, something he didn't want to think about.

"We wait," he whispered back to Todd. Whoever it was had to come out sooner or later.

Todd groaned. Harold knelt behind the tree and dropped the pack. He picked a small glob of yellow pitch off the trunk and tried to roll it into a ball between his thumb and finger. A mistake. The stuff was like glue. He scraped it off with a hunk of bark.

Todd suddenly poked him. "Look!"

Two men and a woman were walking out of the lab building. They strolled slowly, heads down, talking.

From this angle Harold saw something he hadn't noticed on any of his earlier visits. To one side of the dirt driveway, a small parking area nestled in the trees. A beat-up jeep and two other cars were parked there in the shade.

All three climbed into the jeep. Harold heard one of the men laugh. The driver backed around the other cars and sped up the dirt road. Dust hung in the air, then settled. The noise of the jeep's motor faded. Harold relaxed; he'd been digging his fingers into the ground.

"Bet they're going to McDonald's," Todd muttered. Harold put his hand over Todd's mouth. The old man he'd run into last week came through the door of Benny's building. He slammed the door, jiggled the knob, then headed for the lab.

"What're all these people doin' here on *Sunday?*" Todd asked.

Harold didn't know. He'd hoped there wouldn't be anyone around today. His stomach was behaving like a small volcano. His hands felt cold, and the rest of him was boiling.

They waited. A mosquito found Harold's neck. Two crows landed in a nearby tree and scolded the boys for being in their woods. Overhead an airplane motor droned.

When Harold was satisfied that there were no more surprises, he turned to face Todd. "Okay. I go in first.

After I'm inside, I'll signal you." He thought his voice sounded pretty brave. But if Todd weren't with me, he thought, I'd run out of the woods like a scared rabbit.

Todd nodded. He looked a little white. A thin line of sweat had formed over his upper lip.

Harold grabbed the pack. He made sure his cassette player was off. Shoving his glasses higher on his nose, he slipped out of the trees.

He scuttled like a crab until he was flat against the brick wall under the window. He listened for a few seconds. Nothing but Benny sounds. With shaking hands, he dropped the pack inside, then hoisted himself through the window.

He sat huddled on the floor until his heart stopped thudding. Benny stood over his food dish. One hand rested on the wire mesh; the other held a few chunks of monkey chow. His eyes were fixed on Harold.

The place stunk. Whoever was in here hadn't changed the plastic under Benny's cage. The rest of the room looked as sterile as ever.

Harold tried to make himself relax. He felt the way he imagined bank robbers did as they approached the teller, concealing their guns.

Which made him think of his mother. What would she do if she could see him now? He quickly rejected the thought.

Another replaced it, a fact that had been jabbing at the back of his brain: he'd read that some laboratories paid up to ten thousand dollars for a young chimpanzee. Was Benny worth that to the scientists at LAPS?

No, he told himself. Not if they were planning to put him to sleep. But Harold still felt like throwing up. He felt dizzy when he stood up.

He couldn't see Todd when he looked out the window. It would be so simple to just get out of here. Forget about saving chimps and save himself. Instead he waved one arm over his head, stopped, did it again.

Todd stepped from behind the tree, grinning like a kid on a school picnic. He crouched and ran toward the building.

Harold moved his pack so Todd wouldn't land on it. He prayed that Benny wouldn't go nuts when he saw a stranger climbing through his window.

Todd vaulted in and landed on all fours. Benny didn't move. He stared at the boys with bright, unblinking eyes.

If Harold hadn't been so scared, Todd's face would have made him laugh. In the old jungle movies, when an actor comes face to face with a gorilla his eyes get wide and show white. His eyebrows shoot up to his hairline. His jaw drops an inch or two.

Todd did all those things. He looked petrified. "He's so big!" he whispered. "Look at those hands! I bet he could palm a basketball!"

"Shhh!" Harold pointed to the door. "If you hear anyone unlocking it, run."

Todd nodded. He looked around the room. "What's that *smell?* Where's all the other chimps?"

"In the other building," Harold told him. "That old guy you saw coming out of here told me Benny's so mean they can't use him anymore."

Todd stood up and took a hesitant step toward the cages. "Nice monkey," he said softly.

Benny retreated to the back of his cage. He squished himself into a corner and put both hands on top of his head.

"Neat!" Todd said. "We should take him home and make him our pet."

Harold snorted, but he'd thought of the same thing, more than once. His fantasy was to keep Benny in a cabin somewhere. Take care of him until . . . until what? And that's what killed the idea. He wasn't out to *keep* Benny, he was trying to give him his *freedom*.

He moved up beside Todd with the wire cutters in one hand. "Put a few bananas on the windowsill," he said, pointing to the pack. "Make sure Benny sees what you're doing."

Todd did it quickly, first waving the bananas in Benny's direction. Harold thought Benny noticed; he was sitting up straight, staring at Todd.

This is it, he told himself. Go for it. But Harold's body wouldn't move. The wire cutters suddenly weighed a ton.

Todd was standing beside him. "So now what?" he asked.

Harold checked out the cages. They were definitely attached to each other, making one long unit. They would roll easily on those big wheels.

"I cut a hole in the front of Benny's cage," Harold said. The voice was not his own. It seemed to come from some other place. "Then we roll the whole thing over to the window. Benny should take off when he sees a way out."

Todd put a hand on Harold's shoulder. "You sure you want to really do this? We could still leave, you know."

Harold listened, watching Benny's face through the wire. "No. You can take off if you want." He moved to the front of Benny's cage. "Good boy, nice Benny," he whispered in what he hoped was a soothing voice.

He lifted the cutters and caught one vertical wire between the sharp jaws. Benny shuffled backwards, keeping his eyes on the wire cutters.

Harold squeezed the handles. Nothing happened. He tried again, clenching his teeth and squeezing with all his might. Still nothing.

"What's the matter?" Todd's whisper made Harold jump.

"Stupid things won't cut!" Harold felt himself losing control, beginning to panic.

"Let me try." Todd took the cutters and gently shoved Harold aside.

Harold watched the muscles in Todd's arms make smooth bulges as he applied pressure on the cutter handles. When the first wire snapped, Benny got up. He stood as still as a statue, watching Todd's every movement.

"Make a square," Harold said. "Cut all the way down, then across."

Todd moved the cutters down two inches and forced the handles toward each other again. *Snap.* He did it over and over, carving a square the size of a desktop.

Harold held his breath, listening for a key in the door. Any second now about ten cops would burst in with guns and handcuffs.

He felt dizzy, tingly, light and heavy, all at the same time. He wondered if this was the way people felt before they fainted.

"There." Todd stepped back. He had cut through about fifty wires. "Why doesn't it fall out?" He put the wire cutters on the floor and stood next to Harold.

The cut section remained in place. Harold could hardly see the cuts. There seemed to be nothing preventing the square from falling in or out of the cage.

"Maybe we should move the cages now," Todd suggested. "Then take the piece out."

Harold shook his head. "With the cage up against the window, we couldn't get at the wire."

It was a dilemma.

Todd looked around. He walked quickly over and grabbed the long pole from the corner. He pointed it toward Benny and poked the hooked end into the cage. He pulled back, and the cut section came out.

So did Benny.

Harold never saw what happened. Nor did he know which of them screamed. Something black and heavy smashed into him and disappeared out the window.

His head smacked against the cement floor. Red lights exploded behind his eyes. He saw the ceiling through a blur.

When he sat up, Benny was gone. Todd lay next to him. One hand still grasped the pole, sticking through the wire. Todd looked as if he were napping.

Except that his neck and the front of his T-shirt were red with blood.

Fourteen

PANIC FROZE HAROLD. All he could do was stare at Todd's still body. Eyelids, chest, mouth, nothing seemed to be moving. And the blood.

Was Todd dead? What should Harold do? What *could* he do? He felt numb, and suddenly tired, as if a spell had been cast over him.

Then Todd opened his eyes. He lay blinking, staring at the ceiling. He tried to sit up.

"Stay there." Harold put a hand on Todd's arm. He gently removed the pole and set it on the floor. "Your're bleeding."

Harold had never touched anyone else's blood before. It felt warm and sticky and smelled like liver. He swallowed a gag.

"What happened?" Todd looked surprised to find himself on the floor.

"Benny took off out the window. We were in his way." Harold thought he was going to start bawling. "The wire cut you. I don't—"

"Go get someone." Todd sounded scared now.

Harold scrambled to his feet and yanked open the door. His chest and the back of his head hurt, but he ran anyway. He started to cry.

He'd never been so scared in his life. Everything had gone wrong. Todd was hurt. How badly, he didn't know. His mother would find out. Why had he been so stupid?

He wanted to keep on running. Hide in the woods, never go home. Instead he stopped at the first door he came to at the lab. It was locked. He raced around to the main entrance. That door wouldn't budge either.

He kicked it, hurting his toes. Fear burned in his stomach like a hot coal. Then he saw the little white sign: RING BELL FOR ENTRANCE, it said. He could hear the buzzing inside as he jabbed at the button with his thumb.

A voice came from a small opening above the bell. "Who is it, please?"

Harold didn't know what to say. No words seemed to fit the situation. He stared at the round hole.

"Who's there, please?"

He had to say something! "My name is Harold. . . . Benny got loose. . . . He hurt my friend. . . . Todd's bleeding—"

A second later the door was yanked open, making Harold jump back. It was the old man. His face was set in anger as he rushed out of the lab. Then Carrie ran past too, heading toward Benny's building.

Harold didn't know what else to do, so he followed her. He felt totally useless. Worse. Whatever happened to Todd would be his fault. What if he died?

Before Harold reached the other building, the old man came out carrying Todd in his arms. Todd's head lay against the man's shoulder.

Todd looked like a little kid, being carried that way. The old man held a bloody cloth to Todd's neck. His face was the color of skim milk.

Harold followed the old man as he trudged past the lab, toward the house. The girl ran ahead. No one had even looked at Harold or spoken a word to him.

Harold sat alone in the entrance hall of the house. In here it was cool and dim. A little light filtered through the curtains of two small windows on each side of the door. Harold looked around dully. A large oriental rug covered the floor. A small, dark table held a lamp. A tall urn near the door had a couple of umbrellas sticking out of it. Magazines stood in a basket. Straight in front of Harold a stairway curved up to the next floor.

It looked like a cozy room, but Harold felt miserable. He was sitting on a hard wooden bench. To his left, through long red drapes, he could see into another room. There was a TV set, soft-looking couches and chairs, a gray-and-white cat snoozing in a window.

The old man had told Harold to stay put, then carried Todd down a hall and through a doorway. A few minutes later a woman hurried through the same door and shot up the stairs. She came back carrying a basket and a bottle of some clear liquid. She never glanced at Harold.

So he sat. He could hear dull noises coming from behind the door at the end of the hall. He thought about Benny, loose somewhere in the woods. Did he realize what had happened to him? Or that he had hurt Todd? The enormity of what Harold had done made him feel sick.

A clock chimed. How did it get to be one o'clock? His stomach rumbled. When had he eaten last? He looked down at himself. Spots of dried blood dotted his jeans and one hand. He tried to wipe it off on his pant leg, but the blood stuck. He felt cruddy, as if he hadn't washed in days.

Somehow, his earphones were still hanging around his neck. He longed to hear Willie's soothing voice. Instead he heard a door slam. Voices, loud, came from down the hall.

Carrie was walking toward him. "Your friend is okay," she said. "My mother fixed his cut. She says it isn't as bad as it looks." She stood in front of Harold, but she wouldn't look at him. Her hands were jammed into the pockets of her jeans. "My father wants to talk to you."

He followed her down the hall into a big sunny room. Plants stood or hung everywhere. Windows reached from the ceiling to the red tiled floor. An electric ceiling fan moved the air with wide wooden blades.

Todd sat in a rocking chair holding a glass of orange juice. He looked like he was in a TV commercial. Except for his bloody T-shirt, he looked pretty good, even with a Band-Aid on his neck. He smiled at Harold. Everyone else stared at him as if he were some strange fungus.

He counted six other people: Carrie, the woman with the basket, the three people they'd seen get into the jeep. And the old man, looking as if he'd eaten thumbtacks for lunch.

Harold felt his face begin to burn. His hands felt like anchors. Embarrassed, he stared at the floor.

"Todd told us your plan, Harold." Harold looked up. The man speaking had Carrie's blue eyes. He was the tallest person in the room, not quite hiding a soft belly with the loose blue shirt he wore over white shorts. His tan made him look young, but his hair was white. And he was angry.

"What you boys did was illegal, stupid, and dangerous. You'll be expected to pay for the damage to the cage. Harold, I've called your house. Your sitter knows the situation. She tells me your mother is out of town." He paused for a few seconds. "Will you tell your mother, or shall I call myself?"

Harold shot a look at Todd, who quickly glanced down at the floor.

"Yes, I persuaded your friend to give me names and addresses," the man said. "Who tells your mother, Harold, you or I?"

Harold felt about six years old. "I'll tell her," he said quietly.

The man nodded. "Good. I expect to hear from both your families about when and how the cage will be repaired." He stopped and scratched the back of his head.

"First things first. I'm Doctor Fairfield. This is Mrs. Fairfield." The woman nodded at Harold. "And I think you know our daughter, Carrie, and Sam." He introduced the other two people. They were Chip and Laura somebody, husband and wife scientists.

"Carrie told us about your visit here last week. She said you knew you were trespassing on private property."

Harold didn't know if Dr. Fairfield expected him to say anything, so he kept his mouth shut. Someone slipped a chair behind his knees, and he sat. The fan whirred softly over his head.

"Sam told us he ran into you behind Benny's house," Dr. Fairfield continued. "And that you lied to him. Now I'd like to hear your version. The truth would do nicely," he added.

Harold felt like a prisoner on trial. But he had no lawyer, and the jury had already made up their minds. He'd spend the rest of his life in jail. His mouth was stuck shut. He wished someone would offer *him* some orange juice. No one did. They stared at him, waiting.

"I read about LAPS in the library," Harold said. "I was doing a report about chimpanzees, how they're endangered and stuff." It wasn't so bad once he got started. At least they were listening.

"I wanted to see what went on here," Harold continued, keeping his eyes on his knees. "Then when he"—Harold glanced at Sam—"told me you were gonna put Benny to sleep, I decided to let him loose. It isn't fair to kill him!" He raised his voice. "What did he ever do to you?" He hadn't meant to yell. But now he didn't care. They asked for his version, and he'd given it.

Someone coughed. A chair creaked. Finally Dr. Fairfield said something. "Harold, I truly admire the reasons behind what you did today. But you were rescuing a chimpanzee who didn't need rescuing." His voice didn't sound quite so angry now. "We had no intention of killing Benny. Quite the opposite, in fact."

Harold looked up. "But he told me Benny was gonna be put to sleep!" He turned toward Sam. "You said—"

"I said he *should* be put out of his mizry." The old man crossed his arms over his chest. Harold saw the finger that was only a stump. "And I still think so."

Dr. Fairfield sighed. "Sam had a bad experience with Benny when we first got him here. After twenty years in a cage, any chimp would go crazy. That's why Benny was scheduled to go next.

"And *The Times* article you read was written by a misinformed reporter," he added. "Unfortunately."

"We goofed, Pinto." Harold had almost forgotten Todd was in the room. He looked pretty perky now. He wasn't going to die.

Dr. Fairfield looked directly at Harold. "This lab has only one function: to save chimpanzees and get them back where they belong."

"Five years ago we decided to do something about all the chimps dying in laboratories." Laura was speaking now. She looked at Harold through big round eyeglasses. "We take unwanted chimps from labs around the country. They're usually sick, angry, or too old to care anymore, so the labs can't use them. We spend months, even years, bringing them back to health. A few die on us. Others, if they're too far gone, we may put to sleep." She smiled. "The rest are the lucky ones."

Dr. Fairfield broke in. "Our goal is to save chimps from extinction, Harold. Like you, we also care that they're endangered. We're also trying to change that." He smiled for the first time. "If you'd just let us!"

So it had all been for nothing. Benny had been safe all along. Harold had never felt so foolish. "What happens to them? Where do they go?" he asked limply.

"West Africa. The Gambia region." Chip's voice was gentle. He looked kind and wore a curly beard. His eyes blinked rapidly as he spoke. "We send our chimps over as soon as we think they're ready. A group of scientists in Africa takes over where we leave off. They tame local chimps who help our chimps learn how to make it in the wild again. Benny was next."

Harold didn't move. He hardly breathed. Why couldn't this just be a TV show? He'd get a Coke from the kitchen right about now. And there'd be a happy ending.

"Benny would have been shipped in another week," Dr. Fairfield said quietly. "That's why he was kept away from the others."

Sam spoke up from across the room. "And because he's nasty."

"Nasty for good reasons," Dr. Fairfield continued, "and worth trying to save." He looked around the room. "But now . . ."

He didn't have to finish. Harold knew what everyone in the room was thinking. Now Benny would die a lonely death somewhere out in the woods.

And Harold would be responsible.

Fifteen

"CAN'T WE JUST catch him again?" Everyone turned to look at Todd. "Would he go far?"

They all started talking at once, everyone except Harold, Todd, and Sam.

"He could be two or three miles away by now."

"No, he'd stay near LAPS. He knows this is home."

"How long can he last out there?"

"What will he eat?"

"How would we catch him?"

"Would he even let us near him?"

Dr. Fairfield stood up. "We have no idea what Benny is feeling right now, or what he'll do. He's been caged virtually his whole life. He's probably confused and scared to death. I doubt it will occur to him to look for food." He looked around at the listeners. "It's possible that he'd let one of us near him. If we find him at all."

"But he's dangerous," Carrie's mother said. "He's already hurt someone today."

They all looked at Todd, who blushed.

"That was an accident," her husband said. "The boys were invading Benny's territory, and he was probably feeling threatened. We're his family. I don't think he'd do any of us harm."

"Can we help look for him?" Harold knew it was a dumb question as soon as the words were out of his mouth. Hadn't they done enough already, by trying to help?

A loud "Humph!" came from Sam.

Dr. Fairfield seemed to consider Harold's question. "Benny won't let you near him, so I suppose there's no danger in helping us search the woods. The more eyes we have out there the better."

It was decided. Chip called the police station and told them what had happened. The police agreed to patrol the roads and to inform local residents. Harold heard Chip say that Benny was not considered dangerous, but that kids should not be allowed to play in the woods.

Three groups were organized: Carrie would go with her parents. Harold and Todd with Sam. Laura and Chip made up the other group.

They, along with Dr. Fairfield, would carry syringes loaded with anesthetic. There was no way Benny would come back unless he was drugged.

Dr. Fairfield's orders were clear: no one was to approach

Benny, even if the chimpanzee allowed it. If someone spotted him, that person would return to the lab and set off the alarm by simply opening the back door. It would be left unlocked.

"If you hear the alarm, everyone else come back here. Whoever rings it will lead us to Benny." Dr. Fairfield looked at his watch. "It's one thirty. He's been loose about a half hour. We'll meet back here at three o'clock unless we find him sooner."

They split into their groups. Carrie's mother asked Todd if he felt up to tramping through the woods.

"I'm okay," he assured her. The cut was a small one, but all the blood on his shirt made him look like he'd just fought a war.

Harold thought Todd was enjoying the attention. And he figured Todd had told Dr. Fairfield his last name so he could call Mrs. Kinney. He wondered how she'd reacted to the news. His mother's reaction was something he preferred not to think about.

He and Todd followed Sam out of the house. Sam made a beeline for Benny's building, and they had to run to keep up. The day had grown hotter, and the air was still. Harold's stomach groaned. It was part excitement and part hunger.

Inside Benny's building they saw a scene from a horror movie: an empty cage with a hold cut out of it; blood splotches on the floor; wire cutters and that long pole. The smell of chimp dung hung in the air, invisible but foul.

Sam sidestepped the bloody place on the floor and began stuffing his pockets with monkey chow.

110

Benny had knocked the bananas off the windowsill when he jumped through. Harold stuck them back inside his pack. "I have some fruit," he told Sam's back.

Sam grunted. "Came all prepared, didn't ya? Lucky old Ben didn't kill one of you little pests." He stomped out the door.

"What a crab," Todd whispered.

Harold nodded, glad that Todd was with him today. Even after what happened. It isn't so bad being in trouble if you aren't alone.

He hitched the pack over one shoulder. "Let's go before he gets too far ahead."

They spotted Sam about twenty yards away in the woods. He was barreling along, making a lot of noise. Even his back looked angry.

Harold couldn't figure out if Sam hated the chimp for biting off his finger, or if he just hated having to hunt for him. One thing Harold knew for sure: the guy wouldn't win any prizes for congeniality.

"I thought we were supposed to sneak up on Benny," Todd said. "He'll hear that guy a mile away."

Sam had put more distance between them. Harold stopped. "Let him go. We'll never get near Benny following him."

"So what do we do?" They were standing in a grove of young pines. The trees barely reached the boys' chins. Tiny brown birds darted among the branches, pecking at things too small for Harold to see.

Todd snapped his fingers in Harold's face. "Earth to Harold," he said.

111

"I'm thinking. Pretend you're Benny; what would you do first?"

"McDonald's for a shake and fries?"

"Get serious," Harold said. He slid the pack off his shoulder and let it fall to the ground. "I think he'd run like crazy, then get scared and stop."

He peered over the little pine trees toward the more mature, darker woods a few hundred feet to their left. "Then I think he'd hide."

Todd stroked the bandage on his neck. "Maybe he's up a tree."

"Maybe. He'd probably feel more secure with big trees around him." He pointed toward the deep woods. "Like those."

He picked up the pack. "Let's go. We'll walk in a big circle and keep making it smaller."

Todd looked at the sky in the north. A dark mountain of clouds was slowly moving across the sun. "I hope we find him before it rains. And I hope he's inside your circle, not outside."

An hour later, they were still searching. The trees around them towered fifty feet over their heads, making the forest a damp, dark place. The papery bark of white birch trees stood out like blotches of snow. Harold heard a racket in the higher branches. Could Benny be up there, looking down at him and Todd?

The air here was definitely cooler. Harold's skin rippled with goose bumps. He felt like an explorer walking where no one had ever set foot. The spongy ground gave off a smell of decay as they tramped over it.

They stopped under a giant oak tree. Harold thought Todd could probably use a rest. The ground was a lumpy brown carpet of acorns. Harold handed Todd an apple and took one for himself. They ate with their backs against the oak tree, dwarfed by its size.

Harold set his earphones on the pack between them, and hit the Play button with his finger. He kept the volume turned down.

"Who's that?" Todd asked.

Harold told him.

"So who's Willie Nelson?"

"Only the best country singer in the world." Harold dug a hole with his heel and planted his apple core. He wiped his fingers on his jeans.

"The guitar's okay," Todd said, "but he sings like someone's pinching his nose." Todd held his own nose and started singing.

Harold put his hand up. "Shut up. Listen!"

Something was moving and not too far away. Leaves and twigs were being trampled. Whoever it was didn't care how much noise he made. It must be Sam, Harold thought to himself. And here we sit, eating apples and listening to music.

Suddenly Benny came into view, less than fifty yards away. Every hair on his body stood erect. He looked huge and dangerous. He screeched, showing a pink mouth and two rows of ferocious-looking teeth.

Harold felt the back of his neck erupt into goose bumps. He stood up on wobbly legs. He felt like running, but he was afraid to turn his back on Benny. Harold didn't know if the chimpanzee was angry at them or just showing off.

Benny screamed again. He tossed handfuls of leaves and dirt into the air. He jumped up and down, stomping the ground with his big feet.

Then he charged.

When he was so close that Harold could see the red in his eyes, Benny veered off. He stopped and turned, then threw his head back and screeched. He scooped up a branch off the ground and hurled it. Harold thought he was aiming at Todd.

"What should we do?" Todd was standing a few feet away from Harold. He sounded scared.

Harold couldn't answer. All he could do was stare at Benny running around smacking the trees with his fists. This wasn't the gentle chimp he'd visited last week. He had no doubt that this Benny was capable of biting off a finger.

Or worse.

Sixteen

"TAKE OFF," Harold whispered to Todd. "Run back and set off the alarm."

Benny had quit displaying, but his fur still bristled menacingly. He stood hunched forward, apparently listening to Harold's voice.

"What about you?" Todd asked.

"He knows me. Get out of here, will you?" Harold heard Todd let out a breath, then his soft footsteps began to move away.

Go with him, a little voice urged Harold. Dr. Fairfield said not to approach the chimp.

Harold ignored the inner voice. *He* hadn't approached Benny. Besides, Benny needed him now.

Benny seemed to be watching Todd's retreat. His eyes were fixed at some point over Harold's shoulder.

Just then the Willie Nelson tape clicked off. There were no other sounds. Even the birds had stopped twittering, as if they were holding their breath.

Harold and Benny were standing about fifteen feet apart. Benny seemed more relaxed. His fur began to lie flat. He rested his knuckles on the ground in front of him.

"Hey, Benny, want something to eat?" Harold's voice was about three octaves higher than he remembered it. He tried to sound cheerful. "What'll it be, pizza? No? How about a Big Mac? Oh, you want some fruit!"

He bent down slowly and pulled a banana from the pack. His hand shook as he peeled it.

Benny grunted. He shuffled forward, using his knuckles for balance. He stopped a few feet in front of Harold and stared at the banana.

Harold's hand trembled as if the banana weighed ten pounds. "Take it, will you?"

Benny reached out and plucked the fruit from Harold's fingers. He shoved it into his mouth.

Harold watched as he chewed the banana into yellow mush. His eyes never left Harold's face. Even when Harold flopped the pack open to show Benny the rest of the fruit, he watched every move.

Harold backed up, then hunkered down, trying to look like another chimp. Benny sat too, then scooted forward until the pack was between his thighs.

They sat like that, facing each other, while Benny slowly devoured all the fruit. Harold felt his face begin to tingle all over. He was sitting five feet from an ape!

Sitting this close, Harold noticed that the hair on Benny's face was pretty white. His teeth were yellow, and a couple of them were broken. He smelled like no other animal Harold had ever known. It was a deep, sour odor, like a wool blanket left outside for a long time.

"Just think, next week you'll be in Africa," Harold murmured, "playing with other chimps. And no more cages." Now that Benny had quieted down, Harold wasn't afraid. He wondered what Benny was thinking. Did he know what was going on? Did he know he was free?

Harold heard a faint ringing in the distance. The alarm at the lab. Todd had made it back, and the others would be coming soon. What Benny would do then, Harold had no idea.

For now the chimp was stuffing himself with fruit. The change amazed Harold. Ten minutes ago Benny had seemed enraged, throwing sticks and dirt. Now he was at peace, having a picnic in the forest.

Thunder rumbled somewhere above the trees. Harold shivered. They were in for some rain. What would Benny do if lightning began to crash around them?

Suddenly Benny raised his head. A grapefruit hung out of his mouth. Then Harold heard it too. The others were moving through the woods. He started to shake all over.

Was he in danger? Would Benny freak out again, start throwing things? Harold thought he should do something, but his brain had clicked off.

The grapefruit fell from Benny's mouth. He stood to his full height, looking over Harold's head. Harold heard branches and leaves snapping, and voices. He kept his eyes on Benny, half expecting to see him scram up a tree.

"Don't move, son." He recognized Dr. Fairfield's voice. "Just keep doing what you were doing. Show Benny that everything is fine."

They were approaching from behind Harold. He ached to turn around. Benny didn't fly up a tree. He blinked his eyes and bared his teeth in a chimpanzee grin. Harold hoped it was a grin.

Carrie's father walked up to Benny with his hand extended, palm and fingers toward the ground. Then he squatted down and lowered his head. Benny squatted too, and began fingering the man's white hair. Harold knew this grooming was natural among chimps and that they only did it when they felt comfortable. He didn't know they groomed humans, though.

"We're taking you home now, Benny. You've had quite a day." Dr. Fairfield's voice was calm and soothing. Harold wondered if he was afraid.

Benny made a few *whoof* noises. The scientist took one of the chimp's big hands and began stroking it gently. "Okay, Laura," he said. "Keep the syringe hidden. Talk to him."

Laura approached slowly, saying stuff like, "What a messy eater you are!" and "I see you have a new friend" under her breath. She held one hand behind her back. Harold saw her thumb on the plastic plunger of the syringe.

Benny tipped his head and answered her in chimp talk.

His chest was wet with grapefruit juice. Bits of pulp were stuck in the hairs.

Laura kneeled and offered Benny her free hand. He rubbed it against his cheek, making contented noises in his throat.

"*All right!*" someone whispered from behind Harold. It sounded like Todd. Harold's neck hurt from holding it still for so long.

"Now," Dr. Fairfield murmured. "Gently, gently."

Laura brought her hand forward in one smooth motion, not fast, now slow. Benny saw the needle and hooted, but he didn't pull his hand away. While Dr. Fairfield pinched the skin on his forearm, Laura inserted the needle and depressed the plunger.

When it was empty, she pulled the needle out and rubbed the spot on Benny's arm. She and Carrie's father sat and talked to him, holding his hands, grooming his fur.

About a minute later Harold saw Benny close his eyes. He swayed, then toppled forward. Laura and Dr. Fairfield caught him in their arms.

Harold felt his own body go limp, as if he too had been drugged. Then Todd was there, slapping him on the back. The others came forward, cheering and hugging each other. Carrie was jumping up and down.

Chip helped his wife and Dr. Fairfield lay Benny on a litter. With Todd holding the fourth corner, they lugged the stretcher through the woods. Carrie smiled at Harold, then walked with her father and the others.

Mrs. Fairfield waited while Harold gathered up his pack

and cassette player. She picked a leaf out of his hair and patted him gently on the shoulder. "Benny is lucky to have you as a friend," she said.

Harold couldn't believe it was all over. It was two forty-five on Mrs. Fairfield's watch. He felt as if a year had passed since this morning.

They crowded into Benny's little building. Sam had cleaned up the mess and washed away the blood.

Benny lay on a pile of old blankets in a different cage. His eyes were closed, and he was breathing slowly, through his mouth.

After a few minutes Carrie's father herded everyone outside. He said it was better to leave Benny alone while he adjusted to being back in a cage.

Harold asked him if he could come to see Benny before he left for Africa.

"I don't see why not," Dr. Fairfield said. He patted the backpack slung over Harold's shoulder. "Just leave the wire cutters at home."

The boys reached Harold's house under black, threatening, clouds. Mrs. Kinney lay sacked out on the sofa. An opened magazine rose and fell on her chest as she breathed. Her feet were covered with a sweater. About a dozen paper animals stood lined up on the fireplace mantel, watching her sleep.

In the kitchen, Harold opened the refrigerator and stared inside. "You hungry?"

Todd shook his head.

"You telling your mother tonight?" Harold wondered if Todd had any regrets about helping him free Benny.

Todd sighed. "Yeah. But Mom's okay," he added. "Little things don't bother her."

"Will she think this is *little?*" Harold took one grape and shut the fridge door.

Todd smiled, heading for the door. "That," he said, tapping the side of his head, "remains to be seen, my son."

Harold looked down at Todd's bloody T-shirt. "Want to borrow one of mine?"

Todd shook his head. "Nah, I have to change for my lesson anyway." He glanced at the clock. "I gotta take off. See you tomorrow, okay?"

"What kind of lesson do you take on Sunday?" Harold asked through the screen door.

Todd tapped his head again. "Secrets." He pedaled down the driveway, turned left and disappeared.

Mrs. Kinney entered the kitchen as Harold was spreading peanut butter on half a toasted bagel. Her glasses hung on a string over her bosom. She yawned, a little shaky on her feet.

Harold bit into his bagel.

Mrs. Kinney glanced at him quickly, then walked to the sink and ran water into the tea kettle. "Do you want to talk about it?"

Harold finished chewing. "Not really," he said.

"Will Mama be upset?"

"*Upset* isn't the word."

Mrs. Kinney lit the burner under the kettle and turned

around. "What *is* the word?"

Harold sat and tried to think of his mother's reaction when he told her. He couldn't. They hadn't talked much in the past year. Maybe he shouldn't tell her at all. Dr. Fairfield would never find out. Maybe.

Harold put his dish in the sink. "I'll be in my room." He stopped and turned around again. "And thanks, okay?"

While he was changing into clean clothes, Mrs. Kinney knocked softly on the door. "Harold? I'll be leaving now."

Leaving? Why? She never left him alone. He zipped his jeans and opened the door.

"Your mother's home. She's in the kitchen," Mrs. Kinney said.

Seventeen

HAROLD'S MOTHER CAME to his room and knocked. She looked awful. Her shirt and slacks were wrinkled, and her shoes were mud-splotched. A hunk of damp hair hung over one cheek. Her eyes were red and tired-looking.

"Well, we got rained out, and I think I caught a cold. Other than that, I had a terrific time."

Harold sat at his desk, pretending to read his social studies book. "Did you get any lessons at all?" He watched his thumbs torturing the page corners.

His mother yawned and plucked the combs out of her raggedy-looking hair. "Yesterday, yes. We hit about a thousand balls. We putted. We played sand traps till it started to rain. Last night we watched ourselves on video." She blushed. "It was pretty embarrassing, but I learned a couple of things."

An hour ago Dr. Fairfield had asked Harold if he thought he had learned anything today. Harold admitted that he had, a lot. Now it seemed strange to hear his mother saying almost the same thing.

She stooped in front of his mirror and made a face at what she saw there. "Trudy Ford says I can correct my slice if I change my feet."

How do you change your feet? Harold wondered. He almost smiled at the thought of his mother walking into a foot store and asking the salesperson for a different pair.

His mother started to leave the room. "How about some tea and a few cookies?" she asked, turning around.

Harold shook his head. "I'm not really hungry." He felt his heartbeat quicken. Do it, he commanded himself. Tell her. Get it over with. "Something happened today," he said.

His mother stood by the door and looked into his eyes. "Something happened?"

He looked down at his book. "I did something. It's a long story." His heart was going nuts. One eye kept wanting to blink. "You aren't gonna like it."

His mother got busy searching for something in one of her pockets. She pulled out a Kleenex and blew her nose. "Well. Can I have fifteen minutes before we talk? If I don't get out of these wet clothes and under a hot shower . . ."

Harold nodded. His mother left the room. He slapped his book shut and knelt in front of the aquarium. Tammy and Willie hopped over to be stroked.

He felt relieved, and a little angry. The one time I decide to tell her something, she has to take a shower.

Cool your jets, he told himself. She's got a cold. They just drove a couple of hundred miles in the rain. This can wait.

Of course, he'd get grounded. No allowance for the rest of his life. Lose his bike, maybe. But he had to tell her. He wondered whose side she would take.

He tried doing some math. The squares and rectangles all turned into cages. When he looked out the window at the rain, he saw Todd's bloody shirt.

Twenty minutes later he had accomplished nothing. His math book might have been written in Greek. Where the heck was his mother? There were no sounds coming from her room upstairs or her bathroom.

He headed for the kitchen. She was sitting in her robe, eyes closed, holding a mug of tea under her chin. The steam rose into her face like breaths on a cold morning.

Harold wasn't a bit hungry, but he opened the refrigerator anyway. He wasn't sure he could go through with this. He took out the apple juice, then a stalk of celery.

"I'm ready when you are." His mother's voice sounded tired. And a little wary, as if whatever was coming she didn't need.

Harold turned around holding the celery he couldn't have swallowed if he were starving. He set it next to the juice container on the counter. He jammed his hands deep into his pockets to hide their shaking. His eyes focused on a hunk of dust in the corner.

He told her everything. Starting with his English report. Todd. The wire cutters. The people at the lab, Benny, the whole thing.

After a few minutes his voice sounded normal. But he

was shivering. He felt cold, then hot, in waves.

His mother had set her mug on the table. Her hands lay flat on either side, fingers spread, not moving.

Harold stopped talking. He felt weak, as if he'd just vomited. But it was over, and he felt relieved.

"I can see that leaving you home wasn't a good idea." Her voice was flat, as if she was trying to control it.

How do grown-ups do that, Harold wondered, stay all unemotional-looking, when inside they are upset? Kids usually acted the way they really felt. He wondered if his mother could tell how he felt right now.

"Do you realize how dangerous that was? Not to mention illegal? Anything might have happened!"

Dr. Fairfield said almost the same thing, Harold remembered. But he'd stayed calm, and his mother was slowly but surely getting uncalm.

She stood up and leaned forward, pronouncing each word as if Harold had trouble understanding the English language. "I can't believe what you told me," she said, hugging herself tightly. "I just can't believe it."

"It's true."

"I know it's true!" Her voice wasn't very flat anymore. It shook the way Harold knew his did when he was really losing it. "Can you tell me why? Can you? Didn't you think ahead?"

Now Harold was getting mad. His hands became fists in his pockets. "I felt sorry for Benny, all right? I didn't want to see him die." He looked directly at his mother's face. "I wanted to do something good!"

"*Something good?*" His mother looked at the ceiling, as

if the solution to her crazy son's problems were written there. "Breaking into a building? Getting that boy hurt, endangering people's lives?" She shook her head. "I went away because I thought I could trust you!"

Harold lost control "Why don't you stay away?" he yelled. "You're never here anyway! You play stupid golf so you won't have to see me. Why don't you admit it? You hated Dad and you hate me!"

His mother's mouth opened, then closed again. Her eyes showed white all around the blue. "I don't hate you," she said finally. "What an awful thing to say!"

"Yeah? Then why aren't you ever here? Why don't we ever do anything anymore? Why do you spend all your time with Mavis and Cora?"

Harold felt tears hanging onto his lower eyelids. He blinked rapidly. He would *not* cry in front of his mother.

"I work all day." Her voice was breaking. "I take care of this house, alone. I deserve time to myself! Do you think this is easy? *Do you*?"

Harold could see tears slipping down over his mother's face. Her mouth was a wrinkle. "*What do you want from me?*" she cried.

Harold felt his eyes blur. "*Nothing!*" he yelled back. Furious, he swept the plastic juice pitcher onto the floor and ran out of the room.

Eighteen

HAROLD LAY IN BED listening to his mother getting ready for work. The sounds of running water and closing doors punctuated her soft footsteps.

Then she was in the kitchen. Harold wondered if she'd wake him for breakfast. He waited. Soon he'd smell coffee, maybe eggs or sausage.

Instead he smelled only his own breath. He heard a door slam. The Subaru coughed, then started. She was going to work without her coffee!

Harold kicked the covers back and ran into the living room. He pushed the drapes aside and bent his neck to see the driveway. It was empty. The Subaru was nowhere in sight.

She must still be ripped, he thought. He'd been stupid to throw the juice on the floor. But he'd been mad, too, he told himself.

Afterward, in his room, he'd hidden under the bed covers until his hands stopped shaking. Feeling rotten, he'd finally shucked his jeans and fallen asleep.

Now he climbed into them again. He chose a T-shirt showing a mother humpback whale feeding her baby underwater. He avoided looking at himself in the bathroom mirror as he brushed his teeth.

He shoved his books into his pack, slipped in the wire cutters, and headed for the kitchen.

The empty juice pitcher lay on the floor near the stove. The white lid leaned against a table leg. A film of amber-colored juice made a crazy zigzag puddle on the floor.

He stared, unable to believe that his mother hadn't cleaned up the mess. He set his pack on the table and touched the puddle with one finger. The juice had congealed. It felt sticky, like half-dried glue.

He had to step in it to get to the little closet where his mother kept the cleaning things. His sneakers stuck, making little snapping noises when he lifted his feet. He ran hot water into the dishpan and squirted in a shot of liquid soap that smelled like pine trees.

So he'd be late for school. It wouldn't be the first time.

Fifteen minutes later he was out the door. Last night's rain had left the air cool and sweet-smelling. Wide puddles in the street reflected the sky like windows into another world.

Harold found Mr. Gunter reading the comics and sipping coffee. His chair was tilted back and his big work boots rested on his desktop.

He lowered the newspaper when he heard Harold come in. "Hey, how's your mother?" he asked.

Harold laid the wire cutters on the desk. "She's fine," he said. "She went to Syracuse for golf lessons this weekend."

"Well, that's great, Harold. Thanks for returning my cutters. Work all right, did they?" He motioned toward the wall. "How's about hanging them up for me. I'm right in the middle of 'Peanuts.' "

Harold had missed homeroom, so he headed for math. He glanced around the halls for Todd during the rest of the morning, but he didn't see him till English.

Kids were standing around, laughing and talking. Mr. Stanley was handing back reports with grades on them. Harold tried to remember where his was. Probably still in his purple jacket. At home.

Mr. Stanley stopped at Harold's desk. "How was your weekend?"

Harold emptied his pack. "Okay, how was yours?"

"Fine. Got in a little trout fishing. Where's that report you owe me?" He grinned. "I can't give you a grade until you hand it in."

"It's home. I'll bring it in tomorrow, okay?"

"Tomorrow," Mr. Stanley repeated, moving away. Harold turned around. Todd's desk was surrounded by all the guys, as usual.

He caught Todd's eye and waved. Todd waved back, then kept talking with Marty Osborne.

Everyone took a lot of time getting into their seats after the bell rang. Mr. Stanley didn't mind a little fooling around on Mondays. Harold thought he enjoyed the gab sessions as much as the kids did.

"Four of you still haven't read your reports," he told the class. "We'll hear two today and the others tomorrow." He glanced down at his grade book. "Art, Todd, Ronnie, Bob. Who's first?"

A few kids groaned. "I'll give mine," someone volunteered. Harold recognized Todd's voice.

Mr. Stanley smiled. "Thanks, Todd. Come up here and face the firing squad."

A chorus of guys clapped and whistled. Up front, Todd blushed. Harold thought he saw his hands shake. The round Band-Aid on the side of his neck looked like an oversized freckle. He pulled two sheets of wrinkled paper out of his back pocket.

"Neat-lookin' report," someone cracked.

Mr. Stanley gave the wise guy one of his stares. "We're ready when you are," he said to Todd.

Todd unfolded the papers. He looked pretty uncomfortable. "Um, this is kind of short. I was busy over the weekend."

This brought another round of whistles from the back of the room.

"*Bravery*," Todd read. He emphasized the word so we'd know it was his title. "*Bravery means different things to different people. Men who fight in wars are considered brave. Football players are brave. Professional boxers are brave, too.*"

131

Here Todd shook his head. "I think they're pretty dumb, myself." He got a laugh, then continued reading. "*I learned a lot about bravery this weekend. A friend of mine asked me to help him on a project. I went along to see what would happen.*" Todd paused. "*And this is what happened.*"

Harold couldn't believe this. And he couldn't look up, even with Todd standing only about four feet away. He felt a buzzing inside his head.

Todd read more. "*Harold Pinto asked me to help him free one of the chimpanzees from a lab in Watertown. The chimp was old. He was going to be killed, Harold told me. He said he wanted to give the chimp his freedom before he died.*"

Harold wanted to die in his seat. He listened through burning ears as Todd told the class the whole story. Somehow it sounded a lot more believable than Harold's version to his mother last night.

When Todd got to the part about borrowing the wire cutters to rescue his mother from the dog pen, a few kids chuckled. But mostly the room stayed quiet.

As Todd read how he had been flattened by Benny and bled all over the place, Harold could feel everyone holding their breath.

Todd never looked up. He read sentence after sentence in a low voice. He smiled a little when he described how Benny had thrown sticks and dirt in the woods. "*Harold stayed there to calm him down after I split,*" he said. Harold could feel twenty-four heads turn his way. He inspected his fingernails with his face boiling.

132

Todd finished his report by telling the class that Benny was being flown to West Africa to live with wild chimps again. Someone yelled, "*Okay!*" A lot of kids started clapping and stomping their feet on the floor.

After the room quieted down, Todd looked up, right into Harold's face. "I think Harold Pinto's about the bravest kid I ever knew. I'm proud to have him as a friend."

The room was quiet until Mr. Stanley spoke up. "That was excellent, Todd. And you're right, it was a bit short. But good writers know when to stop. You said everything that needed saying, beautifully."

After school Harold headed for Ryan's. He told himself he needed some M&M's, but he knew he was waiting for Todd to come in.

A few minutes later, he did. Neither boy mentioned Todd's report. They ate their candy walking toward Harold's house. Harold asked Todd if he wanted to visit Benny someday after school. "Dr. Fairfield said it's okay."

"Can't," Todd said. "Gotta practice every afternoon this week." He tapped the side of his head. "Big things happening, my son."

"What do you practice, anyway?" Harold asked. "What're all these secret lessons all the time?"

Todd stuffed the rest of his Mounds bar into his mouth. When it was gone, he slid his eyes over to Harold's face. "You tell anyone at school, and you're dead."

They both laughed, remembering when Harold told him the same thing a few days ago. Harold promised by crossing his heart and hoping to die.

"I'm a dancer," Todd said, looking down at his feet. "I take ballet."

Harold stopped walking. "You're kidding."

Todd shook his head. "I've been taking since I was five. I love it. I'm gonna be a professinal dancer before I'm twenty-one."

He poked Harold in the arm and took off down the street. "See you tomorrow, Pinto."

Harold stared after Todd until he was out of sight. Ballet. He walked home, grinning.

Nineteen

HAROLD FIGURED his mother would go to the club after work, so he was surprised to hear a car door slam at four thirty. Then he heard other car doors and voices.

His mother rushed through the breezeway door into the kitchen. She stopped when she saw Harold sitting at the table. He was eating a baloney and cheese sandwich, but it turned to cardboard in his mouth.

His mother glanced at the floor, then the sink. She said, "Thank you for cleaning up." Her voice was back to normal, under control.

Harold poked a piece of cheese back where it belonged in his sandwich. "I'm sorry I threw the juice," he said. "I was mad. It was stupid."

His mother set her purse and carryall bag on the counter. She took a glass from the cupboard and drew some water. After taking a sip she set the glass down.

"Harold, I want you to know that I didn't sleep last night. I thought about what you said—about your father and you. About us."

Harold's ears burned. He didn't want to get into this. But he'd be darned if he'd blow up again.

"I think I did hate Hank when he left. I was so angry and hurt. It was pretty scary." She reached for her glass, almost spilling the water in her haste to take a drink.

"I had to do something with myself or I'd have gone crazy. The bank was hiring. Mavis had been after me to try golf. I figured, why not? You were in school, you had kids in the neighborhood. I had nothing."

She took a deep breath, then let it out. "You were right. I guess I've been trying to stay away from here. Everything here reminds me of your father. Even you."

Harold looked up. He'd forgotten about his sandwich.

"You've grown to look like him. Your hair, the glasses, everything." She smiled, looking embarrassed. "But I never really thought about any of this until last night. I'm sorry I yelled at you. And for a lot of things."

Harold couldn't speak. His mother had never talked to him like this before. Or maybe he just hadn't listened.

Mavis's face appeared in the window over the sink. "Harold! Just the boy I'm looking for. Come around back for a second, honey."

Harold looked at his mother. "I'm sorry, too, Mom. Thanks for talking to me about Dad. I still . . . miss him a lot." He hesitated, then went on. "Do you think I could write him a letter?"

She smiled. "I think he'd like that." There was a pause. "Better go see what Mavis wants."

136

The two women were on their hands and knees in the dog pen. Probably lost an earring, Harold thought. He opened the pen door and stepped onto the velvety grass.

Something fat and furry streaked from between Cora's knees and attacked Harold's sneakers. It was a golden puppy. He grabbed a lace and tugged, growling furiously.

Harold scooped the puppy into his arms. He held it to his chest, feeling the warm little body squirm and jump. The tiny tongue found Harold's chin and licked. Harold laughed and moved his face out of the way.

Cora made baby sounds. "Isn't he adorable?"

"Whose is it?" Harold asked.

"He's yours," his mother said. She was leaning against the pen, watching.

Mavis walked over and scratched the pup under the chin. "Mama's outgrown this pen." She winked at Harold's mother. "Watch out Ruth Goldberg, Tammy's on the move!"

"You have to name him," Cora said.

Harold looked at his mother through the fence wire. "Thanks a lot, Mom. I'm gonna call him Benny."

On Saturday morning Harold raced down Turnback Road. This time he brought his bike up to the Fairfields' house and leaned it against the porch.

Carrie answered the door. She was wearing cutoffs. Her T-shirt had a clump of celery on the front. CELERY STALKS AT MIDNIGHT was printed under the picture.

She looked at Harold with a little smile on her face.

"Your father said I could visit Benny. Can I?" Harold asked, trying to sound friendly. What if she said no again?

"Sure," she said. "But we're just finishing breakfast. Can you wait?"

He sat on the steps, letting the sun warm his face. Was it only a week ago that he and Todd had cut a hole in Benny's cage? Six days, almost to the minute.

Dr. Fairfield told Harold's mother it would cost fifty dollars to repair the cage. Todd had offered to come up with half, but Harold said no. It was his idea to free Benny, and he'd pay for the damages himself.

His mother gave him two bucks a week as allowance, so it would take him about six months to pay Dr. Fairfield. Of course, he'd be broke the whole time, but maybe he could mow lawns to earn a little more.

His mother said Dr. Fairfield had sounded pretty nice on the telephone. They were all nice, Harold realized. They were trying to save chimpanzees. He'd never met anyone who thought the way he did about animals.

He wondered what you had to do to become a scientist who worked with animals, like Chip and Laura. He could ask Mr. Stanley on Monday.

His mother wanted to be a pro golfer. Todd planned to be a dancer. Carrie said she wanted to be a scientist, like her father. What about you, Pinto? his little voice asked. He wasn't sure it would work, but he made a decision: He'd ask Dr. Fairfield if he could help around the lab with the chimps. They wouldn't even have to pay him!

The door opened behind Harold. Carrie had changed into jeans. Her blond hair glistened in the sun. Her lips were glossy with something pink that smelled like crushed strawberries.

"Ready?" She led Harold through a side door of the lab.

They walked down a hall with rooms on both sides. Harold saw Laura talking on a phone. She smiled and waved.

Carrie shoved another door open, and they were in a big room with a cement floor. The room was lined with cages. The first thing Harold noticed was the noise. The second was the smell. He counted over twenty caged chimpanzees.

Chip was rolling up the plastic from under some of the cages. He said, "Hey, you guys. Just in time to help."

They spent most of the morning in the lab making the chimps comfortable. Chip showed Harold how much chow to give each animal. He explained which chimps were sick and how they were being treated with medicines and special diets.

"Are they all going to Africa?" Harold asked.

"Eventually, we hope. A few are pretty sick," Chip told him. "They might not make it." He stuck a finger inside a cage and tickled a chimp on her belly.

Carrie was feeding and watering on the other side of the room. She worked fast, and the chimps seemed to know her, if the excited noises meant anything.

Harold didn't see old Sam anywhere. Just as well, he thought. They hadn't exactly become buddies. Maybe Sam was still mad because Harold had lied to him the first day they met.

Chip brought Harold into a workshop off the main room. Harold saw a lot of tools and smelled sawdust, like in Mr. Gunter's shop class. A large, sturdy-looking crate sat in the middle of the floor.

"Benny's last cage," Chip said, slapping the side of box. "We hope."

The wood was thick and smooth. Air holes had been

139

drilled near the top on each side. Harold put his hand inside and felt soft padding.

"He'll be asleep for the whole flight," Chip said. "Otherwise he'd be so scared he'd hurt himself."

"When is he going?"

"This Wednesday if Laura and I can get all the details out of the way." He grinned at Harold. "Sending a chimp to Africa is a lot more complicated than sending a human. More paperwork. More money!"

They stopped for Carrie and walked outside. Chip unlocked the door to Benny's building, and they trooped in. Harold thought about all the times he'd sneaked through the window. Coming through the door was better, he decided.

Benny hooted softly and sat up. "Drag that barrel over," Chip instructed Harold. He and Carrie filled the food and water dishes, but Chip placed them inside the cage.

"Does he remember me?" Harold asked. "Can I pet him?"

Chip shook his head. "Better not. Any change in his routine can upset him. Sam's been out sick since Tuesday, and Benny sulked for two days."

Benny waited till Chip had locked his door before he moved toward the food dish. As he squatted down, one hand gripped the wire and three fingers poked through.

Harold reached out and stroked one finger quickly. " 'Bye," he whispered. "Send me a postcard, okay?"

Benny looked up, then continued eating his chow. Harold followed Chip and Carrie outside.

Chip went back to work, and Carrie brought two Cokes

out to her front porch. Before he lost his courage, Harold asked the question he'd been thinking about all morning. "Do you think I could help take care of the chimps after school?"

Carrie turned and smiled. The sun gleamed on her braces. "I'll ask my father," she said. "He'll probably say okay. He likes you."

When Harold got home the phone was ringing. It was Todd. "What're you doing?" he asked.

Harold stretched the phone cord to the table and sat. "I went to see Benny. They're shipping him Wednesday, Chip says." He decided not to mention working at LAPS till he was sure. "What's up with you?"

"Practicing," Todd said, sounding a little weary. "Listen, if you're not doing anything, I'm in this recital at our church tonight. You wanna come?"

Harold grinned into the receiver. "You mean I get to see you in tights?"

"Shut up. Will you come or not?" Todd paused. "My mother wants to meet you, anyway."

Harold wrote Todd's number on the phone pad and went to find his mother.

She was planting marigolds in a long golden row next to the garage. Benny raced around, carrying one of her gardening gloves in his mouth. Harold grabbed his puppy and sat in the grass.

"Todd wants to know if I can go see him dance tonight." He scratched Benny behind his ears, feeling the silky fur under his fingers. "He's in a recital."

His mother sat back and wiped her forehead with one

and. "Sounds like fun," she said. "Will you need a ride?"

Harold nodded. "It's at some church. I'm supposed to call him back and get directions."

His mother set a young marigold plant into a hole and packed dirt around the roots. She tapped Benny gently on the nose. "These are not for you, little friend." To Harold she said, "Let me know the details."

Harold went to call Todd. At the door, he stopped and turned around. "Mom? You feel like coming with me tonight?"

His mother looked up. The sun was behind her, making her hair look radiant. "Are *you* inviting me, or was it Todd's idea?" she asked.

Harold smiled. His mother's forehead was smudged with black dirt. Benny raced around her in circles, shaking her glove in his mouth.

"I'm inviting you," he said.